hey, lover

A SECOND CHANCE ROMANCE

DL WHITE

contents

Copyright © 2023 by DL White
    Ebook ISBN: 9798215201459
    Print ISBN: 9798215092507
    No part of this book may be reproduced in any form or by any electronic or mechanical means, including information storage and retrieval systems, without written permission from the author, except for the use of brief quotations in a book review.

COVER ART COURTESY MOON BEY
    www.moonbey.com

foreword

It's been a long time, shouldn'ta left you... but I had to, because life was life-ing, dawg!

Truth time: I haven't finished a full-length project since 2020.

I've tried, but I hit a wall and burnout won and I watched another episode of Bones/Rizzoli & Isles/Law & Order (I love a police show). We all know what life has been like since March of 2020 and while I was lucky to escape with my physical health intact, my mental health has suffered a great deal, resulting in an inability to dream and create. I tried to give myself a break, but I felt weird about not releasing anything new for more than two years and having something fun to entertain the people.

So, I pulled out a little ditty I started in 2021 and decided to finish it.

Young authors: never throw anything away!

This book is not high art or literary genius. It's a fun, sexy story that I wanted to get out.

Hey, Lover, is a second chance romance—a reunion between soulmates who split nearly a decade ago and are brought back together. And yes, I'm so glad you asked— it *is* inspired by LL Cool J's hit, HEY LOVER. Maybe now that song will leave my brain? A girl can dream.

Content advisories for this book include references to cancer, depression, infidelity. There is no death in this book.

This book contains adult language (i.e., cursing), Black lingo (AAVE be all up in this piece) and steamy intimate contact between consenting adults (they do it. More than a few times). It also contains a short relationship black moment (because sometimes characters are silly). It is approximately 58K words and has a Happy for Now ending.

If any of these items are a STOP sign for you, I encourage you to engage in self-care and choose another of my titles or pick up a book by your next favorite author to enjoy.

I appreciate each and every reader, new and seasoned. Please accept my best wishes for the upcoming year and the hope that it is your best year yet!

A last-minute reminder that if you enjoy this novel, tell a friend (or 6) and leave a review. Word of mouth sells books.

XOXO,
DL White

CHAPTER ONE

malik

November 30, 2021

"No! No... fuck! Brandon!"

I dropped a bulky game controller and pulled a set of Hyper X headphones from my ears, looping them around my neck.

"What?" I heard from across the office.

"This motherfu—"

I scowled at the frozen screen, a glitch in the game that I wrote, developed, poured blood, sweat, tears and money into staring me in the face and mocking my existence. I rolled my eyes up to the wood beams in the ceiling of my office and exhaled a breath that was supposed to calm me.

It didn't.

I grabbed my phone and scrolled to a number that frequently sat at the top of my recent calls list. I'd been dialing it a lot lately. My chair made rhythmic squeaks as I swiveled back and forth and waited for Brandon, miracle worker and director of game development, to pick up.

"What up?" His baritone voice boomed through the speaker. He sounded bored. Well, preoccupied. In the background was the ever-present, rapid *taptaptap* of fingers on keys.

"What up?" I snapped. "*What up* with the bug list?"

"What do you mean, *what up* with the bug list?"

I paused, glaring at the phone. On the other end was a patient and practiced silence. I slowed down, took another calming breath, and tried not to grit the words out through my teeth.

"Has the team gone through the errors that the test players sent through yesterday? That is what I mean by *what up with the bug list.*"

"That's what I thought you meant," he said. "You can't be asking about the list I just got yesterday and sent assignments out for fixes today. I haven't even had time to load new code. I'm good, but I'm not that good."

"Something's wrong with the graphics on nineteen. It's pixelated when you grab the charm from the clouds. It's the code, or a corrupt image or... something."

"Something. That's very helpful. You do this for a living, you say?"

"And the lucky gold star trick on seven is still fucked up," I said, ignoring his sarcasm. "Those glitches were supposed to be fixed last week. I can't have bugs, B."

Brandon sighed into my ear. "It's unrealistic to launch a game without bugs. Every game has bugs, Malik."

"I'm not trying to be every game," I argued. "I can't pitch investors, let alone sell games with these big ass *I can't get past a level on this fucking game* glitches. I'm about to put a lot of eyes on us. We've got everything riding on this game, plus so much coming down the pipeline. We need to be flawless. Are you hearing me?"

"Yo, the entire building can hear you," Brandon shot back. "I'm the one wearing the print off of my thumbs. You don't need to yell in my ear about it. We're working on it."

"Okay, then." Sometimes a good tantrum released the right amount of anxiety. Plus, Brandon had always known how to chill me out. "Fix it, then see if you can get a few people to test."

"Malik, you bitch about how much it costs to do a round of demo play every time. It's not worth sending it out right now. We test at major code drops, not every other day."

"We are too close to the finish line to wait for a major code update. Test it— every frame, forward and backward. All the Easter eggs. All the tricks. Every. Level. No glitches, no bugs, no errors. Feel me?"

"Aight, aight. I feel you," he repeated. Brandon was placating me, which was usually the best course of action. I would get my way, but probably not at the speed I expected. "You hear anything about the patent? It's been months. Would be nice if we could show the device when we premier the game."

"Nah," I answered, adding an item to my mental checklist. "I heard these things can take a while, so I'm trying not to be up my attorney's ass about it. I'll check it out, though."

"Aight. Keep me posted. Big things if it goes through."

"You ain't even lyin'.

A year ago, my game studio earned foundational backing from a tech-focused venture capital firm. That funding allowed my team to launch our first game in a series called Galaxy Bros— our take on an updated, future world adventure starring two brothers traveling outer space, collecting coins and charms for points.

Each game was set on a planet. Mercury was a simplistic beginning. The draw of the game were the hidden opportunities to gather additional points, skills and powers. To add to the allure, the brothers were Black, the music was created by Black musicians and even the dialog had drips of lingo relative to our target market. I had dreams of players of all ages becoming obsessed with the Galaxy Bros games.

Emboldened by the success of Mercury, we began work on game two. Venus was an ambitious undertaking. We pulled out all the stops to make a vibrant, fun, interactive game that could be played anywhere.

And that's where the patent came in.

We'd been talking about a game that could be played without dragging a console around. A player's profile and progress would live in the cloud, hosted on a platform and accessible by a dongle. Just like I could take my Fire stick anywhere, all a player would need was a stick and a universal controller.

Design, testing, and development brought us to the point of filing a patent for the Hines Tech Play Anywhere Game stick. It would grant all the Hines Tech games access, which would take our games on the road.

My attorney was expensive and worth every penny. He was confident he could make a case for the stick being an original and useful invention, proprietary to Hines Tech games only. It would be the first step to licensing the device to retailers and expanding its use.

"If you're done with your daily tantrum," said Brandon, snapping me back to real life. "I need to get back to work. And get out of the sandbox. I can't finish the build if you're in there messing with shit," he added. "You'll fuck around and accidentally delete the game."

"I would not accidentally delete the game. I know what I'm doing."

"Ay, man, take a walk. I got notes from you all night long and early this morning, and your attitude is making everybody agitated. I'm working on the bug list. Don't call me again." The line went dead before I could respond.

"If he wasn't my brother, I'd fire his ass," I mumbled to myself, just to say something to someone. With a few taps on the keyboard, I logged out of the sandbox, a temporary space where changes and updates could be seen before a fix to the base code went live.

I dropped the phone to the desk and leaned back, propping my feet up on the corner. The chair squeaked in protest.

Venus would be our first real foray into the market, so we were treating it like a debut with a premiere at Game-Box, the industry's largest independent video game expo. I snagged a spot for our booth and had been riding the team hard to be ready to premiere the game. The goal was to get Hines Tech Studios more funding without giving up ownership of the intellectual property. I had no interest in selling to a corporation for a big payday, then watching them water down and transform the game into looking and sounding like every other game.

Galaxy Bros was different. It would stay that way if I had anything to say about it.

The closer we came to the final phase, the more anxious I was about setting my heart out on my sleeve, and the less I slept. I mostly paced the studio, eyeing the programmers while they updated code, lurking the observation rooms while testers played the game, critiquing everything from graphics to character sounds and the volume of the background music.

I had a small but mighty crew of talent who were underpaid but cared about the product and wanted to be in on the ground floor of something great. They were the backbone of any great game studio, so it was important to keep them satisfied.

And caffeinated. And full. So when I got grouchy, they got free food.

I dropped my feet to the floor and pushed the chair back from the dark wood desk that I had inherited from my father's office. It was fitting, since he was a big reason that I'd been able to launch Hines Tech Studios. I tapped my back pocket to make sure my wallet was there, pulled on a long wool coat to brace against the cold snap in the air and dipped out of my office at one end of an open concept warehouse space.

I wound through the office, passing the bull pen outfitted with low walled cubicles and the lounge, which housed comfortably worn recliners, couches, deep set chairs and two large screen TVs connected to every iteration of streaming programs and gaming consoles. Around the corner from the lounge was the kitchen, an area only used to store whatever junk food the team was grazing that day, endless sources of caffeinated beverages and coffee. Brandon talked me into some fancy brewing system to make his bougie lattes and got the staff hooked on them.

Rebekah, our marketing and graphic design coordinator, was at her desk in a workspace near the entrance. She doubled as a tester and her setup was sweet. Oversize monitors displayed the game larger than life alongside the graphics work she did for me. Her headphones were wireless and Bluetooth enabled, as were her controllers. She preferred as few wires to get tangled up in as possible.

I poked my head over the wall of her cubicle. Her eyes

rolled up to mine, and she tipped her head up to acknowl-edge me.

"How's the feel?"

"Seven's still fucked." She pulled a set of Razer head-phones from her ears as she leaned onto one of the padded armrests on her wheelchair. "It's still freezing when you grab the star, then you can't get out of the sequence. You have to start the level over, then skip past it, then go back—"

"Are we sure it's not the image?"

"Nah," she said, shaking her head. "It's something in the code. Otherwise, that would happen with all the stars. And all the tricks."

"I know nineteen has problems too. Other than that?"

"It's a cool game, bro." Rebekah moved a curtain of micro braids away from her face and flipped them over her shoulder. Her lip and brow piercings lifted when she smiled. "It's a big upgrade from Mercury. It's got a real retro feel, but the updated graphics and functionality make it cool. The glitches are a downer, though. They completely halt play."

"Aight... let B cook and we'll check it in a bit. How are we coming on the booth design for GameBox?"

Rebekah spent a few minutes previewing the latest draft, a shiny purple and blue holographic wraparound image of an intimidatingly beautiful space-themed scene in the game. She used Photoshop to mock up an image of what the booth would look like once it was up.

"Ooh, that's sexy," I swooned, leaning in to get a close look. "I take it we're adding the Venus title and the Hines Tech logo here?" I pointed to a blank spot left of the center.

"Yeah, that's going to be the best spot," she confirmed. "That way, no one is standing in front of it and it doesn't cover up the image from the game. There's enough room to make it bold but simple. Less is more, you know what I mean?"

I glanced at her round, earnest face full of piercings. "Less is more? Is it really Bek?"

"I mean… if we're talking piercings? Nah," she replied. "We don't want to overdo it. Let the game speak for itself."

"I want the Hines Tech logo to be bigger than it is on Mercury. The time for modesty and humility has passed. Let's be loud." Rebekah nodded, then offered her fist for a bump. "Keep at it. B said I'm grouchy and told me to leave. I'll bring back pizza, though. Sound good?"

"Yes!" She gave a Napoleon Dynamite arm pump. "Can you get garlic knots, too?"

"Did I even get pizza if I don't get garlic knots? Let them know over there, okay?"

I nodded toward the tables in the center of the room where the developers were grouped together— four of the best personnel that my investment fund could provide.

I stepped outside, pulling the heavy wood doors closed behind me, feeling immediately harassed by the whip of wind across my face. I buttoned my coat and navigated the sidewalk, wet from a recent downpour. West End Atlanta traffic bustled around me. Cars zipped up the street, pedestrians hurried down the sidewalk, swinging into and out of neighborhood shops.

A few blocks away from Hines Tech Studios was West End Pizza, Pasta and Subs. I'd been eating there since I was a kid. It still looked the same and served the best pizza I'd probably ever have in my life. My dad regularly treated us West End as a reward for good grades. Then there was the time he talked me into taking up a sport, so I joined the basketball team and accidentally made a basket during a game. Though it never happened again, he was proud.

After that season, he let me go back to doing what I really wanted to do: play games and mess around with computers. I always knew that eventually I would marry the two and try to make a living of it.

"Hey, there handsome stranger! Somebody's been a good boy for a few days."

"Don't let anyone tell you I've been a good boy."

My favorite server waddled from behind the bar. Pam always had a loud, gritty laugh and a wink for me. She was very pregnant, and no matter how many times I asked if she was sure she wasn't having twins, she'd laugh and promise that the baby was just big, like his dad.

I pulled out my usual seat at the bar and slid into it. "Every time I come in here, you're rounder than you were before."

"That's how pregnancy works, Malik." She paused when she got close and I bent to swipe a kiss across her cheek. "I was bigger than this with my first baby."

"You make me nervous you're gonna drop that baby, then serve table seven."

She laughed, her silver hoops swinging with the motion. "Boy, you sound just like my husband and my mama. *Shiiittt*," she said, dragging out the expletive, "I gotta stay busy. I can't sit at home, rearranging the closet and boiling bottles."

She palmed her distended belly and sighed. "You can't get back in the building unless you bring back lunch, huh?"

"That's why I found a building near this spot. I need a place to escape when Brandon is getting on my nerves."

"He's getting on *your* nerves? That's not how he's gon' tell that story." Her eyes narrowed, creating crow's feet in her otherwise flawless cocoa skin. "As much as you're down here, you're gonna work yourself out of a crew, Malik."

"I am not that bad, Pam. I am here because I want to be here." Then I grinned, though sheepishly. "He told me to take a walk, though. You got any cinnamon rolls left from breakfast?"

"Don't know about cinnamon rolls. I was short this morning, but I might have something. I'll check right quick, bring you back a surprise."

Pam ambled past me, swaying side to side as she went.

"And then sit down somewhere. Damn. Making me sweat just watching you."

I heard her throaty cackle as she walked through the swinging doors into the kitchen. Across the bar, a flat screen TV flashed images of the round-up from the morning's local newscast. I typically ignored it, since I preferred to get my news online, but something caught my attention.

"... *Atlanta based Parker Enterprises will announce record-breaking earnings in the fourth quarter. The company's new president, India Parker, recently stepped into the role vacated by her father, Bronson Parker. Bronson took the company from a single drive-up convenience stand to a booming, multi-pronged enterprise. The past thirty years have seen the business flourish from a single electronics outlet into storage facilities, standalone convenience stories and retail sales and service kiosks, satisfying every need from mobile phones and tablets to electronics repair.*"

While the reporter voiced the script, the screen filled with footage of Parker locations—Parker Storage, Parker Convenience, Parker Electronics, Parker Repair. Finally, the broadcast switched to a recorded spot from an early morning press conference. Two people winced against the biting wind on the stone steps of Parker Enterprises in front of a bank of microphones.

One of them I knew well.

I used to know her, anyway. I wasn't prepared to see her in living color, right in my face. I wasn't trying to look away, either.

Thick, pillow-soft red lips bent into a wide smile in response to a reporter's question. "Parker Enterprises is as committed to this city as we've ever been," she said, smiling into a microphone. "The same commitments we made when Bronson Parker started this company are the same commitments we strive to meet today. Every charity that we've partnered with, every 5K or food drive we've sponsored, every small business grant that we've issued will receive our continued support. I'm honored to stand in this place, where my father stood for over thirty years. I'm proud to be a Parker and to carry on the tradition of providing Atlanta with all of its storage, convenience, electronic and repair needs. Thank you, Atlanta, for a record-breaking season. We hope to do so much more in the coming year."

India glowed, her espresso eyes dancing like they always did when she was overwhelmed with happiness. A long white wool coat over slacks, a blouse and a jacket, with high-heeled boots to match, did nothing to mask the curvaceous figure that still haunted my dreams.

Hey, lover, I whispered to myself.

The sound of glass against glass broke my reverie. My eyes drifted from the TV to the bar, where a mug of coffee and a slice of cake had been set in front of me. Pam was at the end of the counter, loudly stacking glasses, staring me down.

"Do not start, Pamela."

She shrugged. "I ain't said a word, Malik."

I picked up the mug, still steaming, and took a sip,

stalling to form the rebuttal against whatever Pam wasn't saying.

"You look like you want to say something. She's got her shit together," I said.

"Mmmhmm. India has never known a day when she didn't have her shit together," said Pam. "She was always headed for big things."

"And that's why I'm not about to waste her time when everything is going right for her."

"Reaching out to somebody you used to know real well isn't a waste of time." Pam stifled a snort, but just barely, and went back to stacking glasses. "I'd say you were being a mature gentleman. If I didn't know you're so full of shit, your eyes have turned brown."

"My eyes are brown, Pam."

"Your eyes are *hazel*. They go brown when you're full of shit." She pushed a stack of glasses back, making space to make another row, then went back to stacking. "Or running scared. Does she know you stalk her?"

"I do not stalk her. I can't help that Parker is easy to track online."

"Hmph," she hummed. "You track *India Parker*, not Parker Enterprises. You should call her. Use the press conference as an excuse. This is a big deal for her. You can congratulate her. Open the door. See if she walks through it."

"She will open that door and cuss my ass out," I said, then laughed, filling my mouth with another big bite of sweet cake. I groaned in delight as I finished the piece of cake, but my thoughts remained solidly on India where, admittedly, they had remained during the seven years since our breakup.

I never got over India. That was a well-known fact

among friends and family. My relationship with her, its subsequent demise, my inability to stop rethinking and questioning it... it was my Achilles heel.

I may not have gotten over her, but India was for sure over me.

Two mugs of coffee later, I headed back to Hines Tech, toting an armful of cheesy, saucy, meaty pizzas. And garlic knots because Rebekah wouldn't buzz me in unless I had them.

I sat in on a bug report update with Brandon and the team, then went back to my office to deal with the piles of paper that I'd been avoiding. The amount of paperwork that kept me from doing programming, design and tech work was unreal.

In my pocket, my phone chimed. I pulled it out to see a message from my attorney.

From: T.Clark@StrategicIPLaw.com

To: Malik@HinesTech

Subject: Great news!

Malik,

Just checked the patent website and looks like we have approval! I should get details in a few days, but you can start applying your patent number to any marketing or pitch materials.

Let's talk about licensing options soon.

Attached, find your patent number and my final invoice, payable Net 10.

> Talk soon,
> Tony

I almost couldn't breathe as I turned on a heel and headed back to the group. I held the phone aloft like moving it around would make the email disappear.

"B!" I choked out. "Email from.... from Tony."

"And?" He asked.

"Bro." I blinked and read the email out to him.

"What?" He shrieked, hopping up. "Approved?"

"Approved!" I confirmed. "We can show the stick when we're at Game Expo. We can license it for retail— shit, I gotta update everything. Rebekah!"

"I'm on it!" she called, waving over the cubicle wall. "I had a draft of the pitch deck ready to go in case we got approval. Send me the patent number so I can add it."

"Woman, I swear... when we get on, you're getting the fattest raise."

"Yo, this is dope!" Brandon circled the room, giving hi-fives to anyone in his vicinity. "We are celebrating tonight! You in, M?"

My brain was buzzing so loud, I couldn't think about anything but the piles of work we'd just created for ourselves. "Nah...I've got a ton of work to do now. I basically need to update everything. But take the team. You guys deserve it."

"You sure?" Asked Corey, a computer science major at Morehouse. He scored an internship with Hines Tech for his senior project, and we gained a dedicated student who was willing to work with a ragtag team of developers. "You're the leader of the pack, man."

"I'm sure. You'll have more fun without me, promise.

But be back here in the morning. I'm not entertaining call-outs and I'm not putting up with a hungover staff. Celebrate responsibly."

"Yeah, yeah," came the grumble from the group.

I headed back to my original destination— my office— dialing another number with a grin as wide as Texas.

"We did it, Dad!" I shouted as soon as he picked up the line.

I'd picked up a lot from my father, a wealth management advisor and certified public accountant, on how to work lean to keep the business afloat. I lived in the loft above a renovated West End Atlanta warehouse space, so I didn't have housing expenses on top of a building lease. I drove the same Toyota I'd been driving forever because it was paid off. I didn't take a salary from Hines Tech; I worked freelance contracts to pour the maximum into the team.

So much hung in the balance and weighed on my shoulders.

I popped open a web browser and logged into our Gmail suite. The first few messages were always pings from news sites, some local, some international. I liked to keep a bead on the industry in case we needed to make a quick change in development. Most of the time, I deleted stories without reading. Some I filed away to read when I was bored. Or when Brandon kicked me out of the office.

I sifted through email, filing away every other story. My speaker pinged a notification and a pop-up showed up in my system tray.

Google Alert: India Parker. A print transcript of the morning's press conference popped up on the news wire. I read it, then read it again.

Hey, lover.

My mind was heavy on her, not just because I read everything that popped up about her, but because I still held regrets about the way we split. She'd said she wouldn't wait for me and she hadn't, but we were more than young lovers stumbling around, falling in love, facing the world together. We were friends. I really missed my friend.

Seeing Galaxy Bros about to take off reminded me that India had been around when the game took shape in my mind. I rambled about it. Annoyingly. She wasn't a player, but she supported me more than my brother had. I made her watch me play game after game and she dutifully took notes. Brandon was definitely not watching me play and taking notes.

It had been a long time since we were young lovers spending a Friday night playing video games, eating pizza, listening to music... exploring each other's bodies, hearts, minds, souls.

I opened another browser window and did something I'd told myself I would not do anymore.

"India Parker... marital status..."

I mumbled to myself as I did the hunt and peck into the search engine. A few photos came up—the usual shots plus a few new ones. For the past few years, she'd been connected to Tony Clark, an Atlanta Intellectual Property Attorney.

The same Tony Clark that filed my patent.

India was how I even knew Tony existed, because as flashy and arrogant as he was, he wasn't well known until he started dating India. When my device seemed to be ready to apply for a patent, I reached out to Tony to see if he'd be interested in doing the work. He ignored me, but once I hinted that there could be some money in licensing the device, his tune changed.

I'd met him once, at his office. His lip curled at my jeans and Hines Tech t-shirt. Mostly, our dealings were via email and text, which worked fine for me. The last thing I wanted was to always be looking at the man who spent close personal time with a woman I still loved.

I hoped fate would eventually bring us together, but Tony treated his private and professional life like the separation of church and state. He only invited his more affluent and celebrity clients to parties. The way he always reminded me of payment terms on his invoices told me I was not in that set.

I'd been clocking Tony and India since their first appearance in the Atlanta Business Chronicle. She didn't wear a ring, and neither did he. She laid a possessive hand on his arm in every photo, but they could have been cousins for all the love I didn't see emanating off the page. I didn't see gossip about them— no photos of weekend trips to Hilton Head or romantic Miami getaways. India's Instagram was public, but generic. Her twitter was a personal account, but she wasn't very active on the platform. I created a bland, empty profile to follow her in case she posted something interesting.

I saw right through the charade. That relationship was fake as hell. I was buoyed and even hopeful, knowing that.

I was history to her. We hadn't seen each other, hadn't spoken to each other in years. But things were changing in a very good way for me.

Maybe it was time to heal the rift between us.

I picked up my phone and made a call I hadn't made in a long time and crossed my fingers.

CHAPTER TWO

DECEMBER 9, 2021

"Boss lady. It's time."

I froze, mouth open, cheesy, crispy chip between my thumb and index finger. Kristeena "Steena" Winters, my right hand, my ace, my best friend and Vice President of Operations at Parker Enterprises had just appeared in the doorway of my office, fists planted on stylish, curvy hips and a scowl on full, glossy lips.

"You sound like what's-her-name on that old Steve Harvey show. You know... when he played the teacher? Mr. Hightower?"

Steena stared, her expression blank. "What are you talking about?"

I popped a Cheese Curl into my mouth and glanced at my watch, then my phone, then my calendar. "Nevermind. Time for what? I just caught up."

"For you to take your stubborn tail up to *your* office.

Bronson officially retired last week. He's not coming back to snatch it from you."

I dug into the half-empty bag of Cheese Curls with disinterest in whatever Steena was talking about. I forgot to ask Evelyn, my father's...*my* executive assistant, to order lunch, so I swiped a bag from Steena's drawer stash and crunched through a conference call.

The press conference we held ahead of our upcoming earnings release was a great moment to celebrate our success, but an unnecessary move to brag about good numbers before the report was final in January. Bronson Parker, however, always got what he wanted. His last act before packing up his office and stepping away from the business was to give an official hand off and send a message of confidence to the community and the staff. He wanted no question that he had left Parker in great hands.

If only everyone agreed that the business was in great hands.

Since it had become abundantly clear that I would succeed my father as CEO, his executive staff, charged with keeping Parker's divisions running efficiently, had regressed into children sulking in a corner. They reluctantly attended my meetings. When my father was not in attendance, they were quiet and sullen or argumentative.

I didn't mind Dad still hanging around, because it meant that I didn't have to move upstairs yet. But I'd finally told my him that the slow goodbye wasn't doing either of us any favors. Part-time hours and floating around the office made it seem like he was still in charge.

I asked him to set a date, make retirement official, make the official hand off, and then don't step a foot inside Parker Enterprises until the annual Directors meeting in the spring.

He'd been gone a week, and I had yet to work on the executive floor a full day.

Steena stomped a well-heeled foot. "Why are you holed up in this little ass office and not upstairs on the executive floor, working in the corner office that you earned?"

"This is not a little ass office," I argued. It was actually a pleasant space to work, the size of two offices with a side lounge, a conference room, and a kitchenette. I'd worked in this office since I was promoted to VP of Operations eight years prior. "Technically," I added, "this office is in the corner."

"On the wrong floor. Do I have to get security to manhandle you?"

"Knock it off," I told her, but I was laughing. "Don't make me tell Tony about you."

"I'm not scared of that little man."

Steena was over a foot taller than the man who was mostly a steady date and a passably good time. She would get more joy out of taking him down through lively debate. She finally stepped into my office, planting herself in the guest chair.

She reached for the bag and scooped a few Cheese Curls with the tips of her nails before pushing the bag back toward me. "Speakin' of Tony, he didn't RSVP for dinner."

"Oh..." I winced, looking away. "He told me this morning he can't make it. His Oakland clients scheduled a deposition. With the time zone difference, he'll be on Zoom while we're making our toasts."

"Now ain't that some shit," she said, a little too loud for my liking. "It's your celebration dinner, and it was not a surprise. He knows this is a big deal, right?"

"Yes, Steena," I answered, nodding with a derisive chuckle. "He knows this is a big deal, but I can't insist that he tell his partners he can't handle a deposition because his girlfriend had a good year at work."

"And that's another thing." She chewed and pointed a cheesy, dusty finger at me. "It's been three years and people are talking."

"About what?" I asked, pretending not to know what Steena was getting at, even though it was her favorite subject lately.

"You know what. Your ring finger should be weighed down with a ridiculous diamond. I should be going blind from the glare right now. I'm going to say something the next time I see him."

"You are not," I said, stacking folders on my desk and unearthing my day planner. I frowned at the mess of scribbles across the page. Hopeless. "You know we're not like that. If I wanted to marry Tony, I'd be married to Tony."

"You don't want to get married. That's what you're telling me?" She stared at me, her lips a straight red line of Fenty across her face. "Like you don't watch all them bridal shows and follow that African wedding gown designer on Instagram—"

"I don't follow Alonuko."

"Well, you look at 'em and send me the gowns you like. By the way, she just posted the Look book for next year. The dresses are gorgeous!"

"Beautiful gowns," I quipped. "It's not that I don't think about marriage. Look at what's been happening the past three years. Like I would have had time for a serious relationship while shadowing my father so I could take over. Tony and I are not headed down anybody's aisle. Lord help him if he lost his mind and asked. And don't let it be in public."

I suppressed a shudder. Tony's personal style leaned

toward showy, visible name brands and possessions that loudly boasted his tax bracket, from his Lamborghini to his diamond encrusted Rolex— neither of which he could really afford, but in the circles he wanted to circulate, appearance was everything.

Though we'd come a long way, the Parkers were not always well off, able to buy whatever we wanted, where money was not really an object. I loved nice things, but the flashy, shiny facade did nothing for me. I wanted nothing Tony thought I would like.

"It won't look funny that your man of three years is not at your celebration dinner? What's Bronson going to say?"

"I'll tell Dad he's working. He loves a man that works hard. Leave it alone, Steen."

I snatched the bag of Cheese Curls and rolled the top down so I couldn't eat anymore, then tossed it at her. "Take these before I finish this bag. My trainer is going to kill me when I make it back to boot camp."

"She'll know anyway, and then she'll pull out that tired lecture—"

"You can't outrun a poor diet," I recited with her. "Can I see what you're planning to share in today's staff meeting? I want to anticipate what finance is going to throw at me about next year. I have some ideas and I want to know how much money to allocate."

"Ideas?" she asked, her brows riding high. "Like... new things? You know the staff doesn't like new things."

"Like a new CEO?" My laughter dripped with sarcasm. "Unfortunately, their new CEO wants to do new things. We're leaving so much money on the table playing it safe. It's worth it to explore options. Besides, a new thing to focus on will keep me out of their hair."

She and I chatted over the proposed presentation that

afternoon. She left my office with the empty bag of Cheese Curls, but not without threatening to call security if I didn't report to my office upstairs.

"Go upstairs," she ordered. "I'll throw you over my shoulder and carry you myself if I have to. Don't let them old people scare you."

The balled up post-it note I lobbed just missed her as she ducked out of my office and around the corner. I swiveled around to the monitor and surveyed the mess I'd made of what was now a too-small desk.

Truth be told, I hadn't moved to the executive suite because I could hide on this floor. The older staff that had been with my father for years liked the quiet, stuffy blandness of the penthouse office suites and rarely visited the floors below.

My father was a great man who exceeded every expectation set for him. He left a legacy of greatness that I admired— worshiped, even. Stepping into his shoes made me excited…and nervous that I wouldn't be able to carry the mantle. The grumpy men and women that made up the executive team were set in their ways with old school ideas. They were none too pleased that he turned his company over to his daughter.

Never mind that I'd been running the company in his shadow for a full year before he turned over the reins, or that I'd been making moves and decisions since I took over that expanded our profile and multiplied our earnings.

By all means, continue to be angry that Bronson Parker retired and left his little girl in charge.

The delay in moving upstairs meant that Steena was still working from a small office that was beneath her status. She would inherit my old office when I moved, and she was on the verge of complaining. Time to step into this moment, and act like a real CEO. I resigned myself to packing up a few items, my slim laptop and my coffee mug, and traveling down the hall to the elevator.

On my old floor, there was... *commotion*. Phones ringing, printers chugging, employees in the break room laughing surrounded by 80s style prints on the wall and faded carpet and beige cubicles.

On the executive floor, it was prim and proper niceties in the kitchen, a whisper quiet printer in the copy room, polite greetings accompanied by fake smiles from people who had been wealthy and elite so long that they forgot how to be people.

High art. Plush carpet. Muted colors, painted vases with silk flowers on windowsills, hushed tones. It was so *quiet*. I hated it up here.

I headed to my father's... *my* office the corner suite on a floor of office suites. I couldn't get used to coming to this floor, walking to the office at the end of the hall and not seeing my dad behind the desk, leaned back with the phone against his ear and his feet propped up and crossed at the ankles.

Evelyn manned a desk in a cubicle right outside of my office. She ended a phone call and stood, smoothing her silver bob behind her ear and pulling a pair of glasses from her eyes. She was always so smartly dressed, head to toe. Today she was in a black Chanel suit, white silk blouse and low black pumps, accented by glittering diamonds in her ears, in the pendant at her neck and the rings on her fingers. Ms. Evelyn was always the picture of *well-taken care of.*

"Good afternoon, Ms. Parker." Her voice always held a silky tone that warmed my insides—comforting, but also authoritative. Today I detected a ribbon of amusement. "I see Ms. Winters was able to talk some sense into you. It's nice to see you where you belong."

I scowled, passing her desk. "Yeah, you all made your point. And please call me India. I don't need formality."

"In private, I'd be happy to. In front of the team, it's always Ms. Parker. I won't give them any opportunity to disrespect you. Stay woke, as my grandchildren say." She grinned, seeming proud of herself before quietly admitting, "I don't know what that means, but it seemed fitting."

I tried hard not to laugh, but I had to. "Can you call the interior design firm and have them come out? I need this office redecorated immediately because... *damn*. It's so Bronson Parker in here."

I shuddered at the masculine furniture, the dark wood, the executive leather chair, the serious carpet, the bar service full of brown liquor. I was a red or white wine kind of gal and never at work. I could stand to have a smoothie bar in my office, though.

I dropped the items I'd been holding on the desk and muttered, "I feel like I need a cigar and a splash of Old Spice."

Just as I had settled into the chair and spread my work across the now appropriately wide desk, Evelyn was back with Steena on her heels. I didn't see her so much as heard her, because she was hidden by a giant bouquet of long-stemmed deep crimson lilies in a crystal vase.

My heart dropped into the pit of my stomach. These particular flowers—giant, gorgeous Calla Lily blooms— were hard to find. You had to know which florist to call and they had to be flown in. I only knew one person who would care enough to hunt down the flowers that I loved above all others. I rose from my chair, eyeing the bouquet and reminding myself to breathe.

"I could have brought them in here, Evelyn! I swear you just stick your nose in where it doesn't belong—"

"Let me do my job, Ms. Winters!"

"Ladies!" I interrupted. "When... when did those come? Who are they from?"

"I grabbed them from the receptionist a few minutes ago," said Steena. She grabbed the card and handed it to me.

I pulled the card from the tiny envelope. '*Congratulations on your success. Best Wishes*' was scrawled in handwriting that I didn't recognize. I turned it over. It wasn't signed.

"Anthonius Lovell Clark has never sent you flowers at work," said Steena. "Maybe he's feeling guilty about missing dinner?"

"Uhm...thank you, Evelyn." I gave her a small smile and added, "Could Steena and I have the room, please?"

She nodded and marched out, closing the door behind her.

I handed her the card. "You're right. This isn't Tony's style. He'd want to make sure I knew they were from him, because he doesn't really do flowers."

She took the card, read it, then flipped it over to confirm it wasn't signed. Her eyes popped back up to mine. "Who else would send you an enormous bouquet?"

My brothers, Ian and Isaac, were older by a few years and co-owners of a Parker spin-off, Parker Cares, a lawn and home care company. They were too busy to hunt down my favorite flower from an obscure plant shop.

My father and his wife would sign a card.

My mother was more of a '*Here's a designer bag, Pookie. Proud of you!*' kind of woman.

Besides, they'd sent well wishes and gifts already.

"Steen. I think these are from Malik."

Her eyes widened in surprise. "Nuh uh. Like...your college ex-boyfriend, Malik?"

"Don't pretend you don't know who I'm talking about. We only know one Malik."

"And we haven't seen him in so long I wouldn't know him if he was standing in this office. I don't want to sound like a hater—"

"But you're about to."

"But you haven't heard from Malik since the day he broke up with you for no reason and walked out of your place. Honey, it's probably Tony. It *is* a big deal— he knew you would love these, and he just forgot to sign the card. Could be he's turning over a new leaf, about to get serious."

But I didn't *want* them to be from Tony.

My very casual relationship of the last few years with Tony Clark made sense on the surface. He was HBCU educated, in good standing society-wise and a catch if you believed the gossip around Atlanta. The role of our relationship was, primarily, to keep my parents off my back and to have a handsome man on my arm when I was invited to a social event. We were both busy executives with a steady need for a social companion. We enjoyed each other publicly, and privately had some fun, but we didn't have a *sends congratulatory flowers* kind of arrangement.

To Steena's point, maybe he was trying to have a different arrangement. Which would be a problem because I wasn't trying to change up our arrangement.

In fact, if these flowers were from who I thought they were from, our arrangement was about to expire with no notice. Against my better judgment, my heart soared with the hope that it was Malik.

I quickly squashed it, though. It took me too long to

stop thinking about him every day, to stop wishing he would reach out, to reverse our split, to admit it had been his biggest mistake. He hadn't. It had been seven years. No sense in pretending he even knew who I was now.

The watch on my wrist vibrated. My phone and laptop chimed a reminder about our meeting.

"You're probably right. I'll go see Tony before dinner. Maybe he can take a break from his video deposition, and I'll thank him properly."

The staff of Parker Enterprises gathered in the main conference room around an oval table. The leaders of each of Parker's enterprises were represented—Presidents of Parker Storage and Parker Retail, which operated our electronics, repair and convenience operations, as well as our company divisions- marketing, human resources, finance, legal and operations.

I took my seat at the head of the table, a proud moment for me, having always seen my father in this chair. I was coming into my own and tried to exude an air of confidence.

Never let them see you sweat, or whatever that deodorant ad had said.

"The beginning of the fiscal year is coming up quickly," I said, opening the meeting. "I want to go into it with an aggressive plan to source and implement a new offering. It's the perfect time to take advantage of a hungry market. I really want to play to the demographics that we don't serve well. If you'll look at slide one of today's presentation, I've included a breakdown of—"

"India...if I may?" Quinn Hadley, VP of Business Development, piped up from the other end of the table. "Is this meeting really necessary?"

Quinn had been with my father the longest. He'd seen a lot and likely felt that he should have succeeded my father, despite always knowing I was being groomed for the role.

"What about this meeting isn't necessary, Quinn? This is annual planning, and everything starts with the numbers. That doesn't change simply because there's a different Parker at the head of the table."

"Well, I meant we expected you would be more like the *face* of Parker. You know, a figurehead with the Parker name. I assumed that day-to-day business and new developments would be run by the staff at this table."

"Why would you assume that? Certainly nothing my father has said or done in the last three years indicated I would not take an active role in running this company. I don't understand what you're getting at. Or maybe I understand, but I don't like what I'm hearing."

"Maybe I'm just speaking for myself, but no one is looking for Kiosks 2.0 from you."

"Why not? The kiosks are already profitable," argued Steen. "We're six months ahead of forecast. India might know what she's talking about when it comes to pushing us in a new direction."

"Okay, sure. Your little idea has made us a few dollars." I rolled my eyes at his characterization. My *little idea* had transformed the business and earned each member around the table a nice bonus. "I'm just saying, maybe you should ride that for a while. At least through the coming year. You don't need to be in the trenches, rolling up your sleeves, working hard."

He chuckled, pumping his arms like he was running. "All you need to do is spend your paycheck on maintaining the pretty face, buy designer bags and shoes so people know we pay you well, stay out of the news and show up for interviews and photo shoots. The press conference turned out nice, right?"

"Nice. You think announcing record breaking earnings for our company, something I had a hand in orchestrating, since I have seen none of *your* ideas hit the market, Quinn—was...*nice*."

"Well, let's be honest here." An evil, joyless smile crossed his lips. "If my father owned the company, I could push a basic idea that any intern could come up with, by the way, out to market, too."

I heard the air physically suck out of the room. The tension was so thick, so palpable, it was like swimming through soup. I fought myself to not break into a sweat.

Steena rose to her feet, pushing the chair back so hard it rolled to the wall. "What is your problem, Quinn? You need to glue that useless flap in your face shut."

"Or what, Kristeena? You'll get your bestie to fire me? Replace me with another one of her unqualified friends?"

Steena lunged across the table. Quinn arched back in his seat, eyes wide.

"Enough!" I shouted, loud enough to silence whatever Steena had been gearing up to shoot back. "Ms. Winters! Have a seat."

She glared, then a grabbed her chair and rolled it back to the table. She resumed her seat, till shooting daggers at Quinn. He eyed her, warily scooting back up to the table.

"It looks like I need to clear the air. I am only going to make this speech once, so listen closely."

I stood, pulling at the hem of my winter white peplum suit.

"My name is India *Parker*. I'm President and CEO of Parker Enterprises and that means that this company is in my very capable hands. I have advanced degrees and years of experience with this company. I know every nook and cranny of this business. I grew up knowing that this role, the very spot I'm standing in, was designed for me. I'm not a little girl playing office. I eat, sleep, and breathe Parker."

I paused a beat to breathe, to settle the hammer of my heart against my rib cage and to glance at Steena for support. Her lips held a hint of a smile and a brow lifted.

"It's my intention, in taking over Parker, to bring innovation to a company that still operates like it's the 90s. If we don't evolve, we will stagnate. More agile companies will outperform us and eat us alive. We need to streamline our processes and we need to turn our minds toward how we do business in the future. That is my top priority, and I will replace leaders who don't share a desire to achieve these initiatives. I do not follow the direction of this team; I lead it. If you don't want to join me in those endeavors, I welcome your resignation."

My eyes roved the room. Not so secretly, I hoped someone dramatically stormed out, but there was no such bravery, and I knew there wouldn't be. There was too much money, too much time, and too many stock options appreciating in value around that table.

"I hope you all heard me clearly, because if we have to have this discussion again, it'll be at your exit interview with Ms. Billings from Human Resources."

She quickly bowed her head, her jowls sagging. Every

person, save Steena and Evelyn, stared at the marble etchings on the conference room table as if they were interesting.

I resumed my seat and nodded to Evelyn to advance the presentation slide.

"We have a full agenda, so let's continue. As I was saying, look at the demographic breakdown on slide one."

CHAPTER THREE

THE LAST DAY I SAW HER WAS BURNED INTO MY MEMORY AND haunted my dreams. The hurt in her eyes, the downturn of her mouth, the slump of her shoulders. She put on a brave front, but she was not okay.

It was a crisp, early fall Saturday morning in October 2014. It was one of those mornings we loved to spend in bed whispering sweet things to each other, enjoying just one last taste before succumbing to the day and our responsibilities.

The conversation between us that morning, though, wasn't sweet. And while I'd think about it for years afterward, it wouldn't be my favorite memory.

"I don't understand, Malik," said India. Her voice quivered as if tears were on the horizon and just barely being kept at bay. "It doesn't make any sense. We hardly even fight. What did I do?"

India stood in the marble tile foyer of her condo in a city center mid-rise tower, arms crossed and head cocked. The luxury space was still so new, paint fumes lingered in the air. She was still in her workout gear— a sleeveless pink top with the Nike swoosh across an ample chest, matching leggings, and pristine white sneakers.

Her appointment as Vice President of Operations at Parker meant she could take the next step on her detailed five-year plan: move out of the Parker family home into her own place.

Part of the plan had been for me to move in with her, but the more I thought about it, the less I agreed it was a good idea. I'd come by, not to pick up a key and celebrate her new move, but to break the news that I was a taking a step back while I had the nerve to do it.

"You didn't do anything, India. For real, it's not you," I told her, wincing as the cliche left the tip of my tongue. "It's me. It's all me. I need some time. Some space. My dad isn't well. My company is failing..."

I pushed out a heavy, emotion-filled breath. "I'm not where I want to be and I don't have the time or the energy to keep this going. I can't make you happy right now, and—"

"Since when does another person make us happy? I'm happy when you know you can lean on me. Glean strength from me, like I get from you when I need it. You think I don't know shit's rough in your life? I'm here, though. I'm not running away because you're going through something hard, something life changing."

"I know you're not running. And I love you for that. But ..."

My gaze had been on the floor because I couldn't watch her eyes pool with tears and the edges of her mouth draw down. I flicked my eyes up now, though. I had to be brave enough to take this step. Or bold enough to be this dumb.

"But you should. You should run."

Her expression was a mix of shock and mocking. I didn't

blame her. I sounded silly to me, but I had to do this. For her. "I should run from you? From *you?* A man I love and would fight for and want to see win? You hit a snag in life and I—"

"Should run!" I cut in. "Yes, run. I can't do this. I can't match your energy and I don't have your optimism and your passion and a five-year plan. I barely have a one-year plan. Life ain't been the crystal stair that it's been for you, and I can't live off of you, India. I refuse."

"So this is all some kind of macho, *my woman can't earn more than me, can't support me* bullshit? What year is this?"

"I don't have shit, India. I mean it. And I can't..." I sighed, exhaling from the depth of my lungs. "I love you so much. You don't even know. I love you enough to let you go. I need time to get my shit right."

Her mouth dropped open, a caustic, angry reply set to fly. I was ready to hear it, especially after I mentioned the cushioned life she had led. But she didn't. She pressed her lips together, bowed her head, and gave a resolute nod.

"Fine," she bit out through teeth clenched tight. Then she stepped around me, grabbed the doorknob and pulled, swinging it open. "If that's the way you want it, take all the time and space you need. Work out this episode you're going through, where you seem to be angry about where I am in life. I might not be here when you realize that you're a grownup in a mature partnership where two people who love each other support each other through thick and thin. Good times and bad. Salaried and hourly. They don't run when it gets hard."

"I already know that. I wish you could understand that it's not about your stage in life or the money you make. It's about me feeling like you deserve a better man. You deserve a man who can't walk out of this door. And I'm sad to say it, but…"

I turned and walked through the open door, only pausing long enough to finish my sentence. "I'm not that guy."

I was halfway down the long, carpeted, whisper-quiet hallway on the way to the elevator before I heard her apartment door close. Not even a slam. Closed quietly and softly.

That wasn't a sign of her emotional state. I knew she was raging and already on the phone with her best friend, Steena. I deserved every insult they were hurling at me.

It hurt me to hurt her, but it hurt a hell of a lot less, I was sure, than it would have when I didn't have time or emotional capacity… or money… to participate in the college friendship turned post college love story.

We had fallen in love slowly. So slowly that I hadn't realized how unequal we were.

It was just me, Brandon, and Dad, a widower whose cancer was whittling him away a little each day. I was also the beleaguered founder of a tech company on its last leg and I'd just been turned down for a small business loan— things I'd kept from India because I didn't want her to think I wanted her or Parker to bail me out.

I was about to be evicted from my apartment and, instead of moving in with India, was moving back into my childhood bedroom to avoid my belongings being put out in the street. My car only still worked because my brother was a mechanic. I wore sweats and misshapen t-shirts and too infrequently shaved the scruff of beard that accumulated in wiry patches across my chin.

I didn't see a way out without India wanting to help. I could not… *would not* drag her through hell.

India was privileged, brilliant, funny, and stylish. The

Parker family, from the grandparents to the youngest grandchild, earned graduate degrees and was well-off. Even before taking roles in the family business, her father always set India's jobs up for her. As the only one of three Parker children interested in taking the mantle, she always knew she would inherit Parker Enterprises. If her family wasn't already side eyeing me and suggesting more suitable, wealthy, established matches, it would begin soon.

India would defend me with her dying breath. I didn't want that for her. I didn't want her to have to dig me out of a deep, depressive hole. I wanted to save myself, so she didn't have to.

I ducked into my car, huffing sadness and disappointment into the air as I inserted the key into the ignition. There was no time to reflect on letting go of the best part of the last few years. I had to take my father to his chemotherapy appointment, then care for him while the side effects of his disease and the so-called cure ravaged his weakening body.

And then I had to figure out how to save my company. We wouldn't last the year if I couldn't.

When I started seeing her with Tony Clark, I thought she might be moving on.

He was closer to what her family would want for her, closer to what she deserved, and if she kept moving in those circles, she would eventually find someone to fall in love with.

But what kept hope alive, somewhere deep down

inside, was the lack of light in her eyes, the smile that never went past her lips, the closeness I didn't see between them.

While I didn't have it in me to keep in touch, I always knew what was going on with her, courtesy of my *India Parker* google alert.

And slowly but surely, I dug myself out of a black hole.

After several rounds of chemotherapy and a drug trial, my father's health rallied, and he stabilized. He began gaining weight back and as his health improved more, he made sweeping changes to his lifestyle. He retired, sold the house and everything in it, liquidated his investments and moved to an assisted living community at the beach.

"And what happens if you get sick again?" Brandon and I had asked while watching him blow up his life.

"Then I get sick," he declared. "I'm not doing treatment again. If I go, it'll be at the beach. On my terms." Clifford Hines had made his decision and followed through on everything he said he was going to do, including sowing into our futures.

"You can put this to better use than I can," he told me when he cut me a check for the fund that I would have inherited. "And you can use it now, so take it. Do your thing. Make me proud."

Putting myself back on the right path took time. Time that stretched into months and years, and suddenly it had been seven years since I told India that I needed space.

But I missed her. I missed *us*.

And I could see it in her eyes— she wasn't happy.

I was in a much better place, and the future looked unbelievably bright.

I opened a web browser and brought up the website for Parker Enterprises, Inc. I clicked on the Leadership tab and smiled at the glamor shot of India, with the title President & Chief Executive Officer under her name.

Damn, I was proud of her. I opened an email and tapped out a brief note.

I contemplated saving the email to drafts, but decided not to be the same weak dude I was years ago and hit 'send'. The email disappeared with a *whoosh*.

She would either ignore it because it had been seven years and she was exercising her right to still be angry with me.

Or she'd respond.

Either way... the ball was in her court.

Shit. I began to sweat.

CHAPTER FOUR

I WAS STILL FUMING AFTER MY MEETING THAT WAS, ACTUALLY, A bust. Most of the staff were quiet, stiff jawed and non-committal about the upcoming fiscal year. We did agree to put money toward updating our in-store point of sale systems and begin an upgrade of our accounting software, so I won a few minor victories.

I wanted to get out of the building and have a glass of something sparkling and alcoholic with Steena, but she'd left early to get ready for dinner.

"I'm leaving, Evelyn," I said, pulling my office door shut. "Feel free to be right behind me."

She looked up from a stack of cards and envelopes, pen poised. "Thank you, Ms... India. William picks me up on his way home. May as well finish addressing these company holiday cards. You know how slow the mail runs this time of year."

"Goodnight, then." I heaved an exhausted sigh as I passed her desk.

"India..."

My shoulders slumped as I turned slowly, already knowing what I was about to hear. "Yes, Evelyn?"

"Why do you look like my grand babies when I'm about to scold them?" She asked with a laugh that warmed my heart. "You would have already heard it if I had any argument. Now, what you had to do today? That was bold, child. But it needed to be said, exactly how you said it."

"Really?" I turned back toward her desk. "You... you don't think I was harsh?"

"Those people needed to hear it. They're acting like spoiled children and I hope some of them decide to move on. And I hope you're ready to stand by those words to let them go if they can't get on board. You have my full support, Ms. Parker."

She winked, then added. "You know, every day that passes, you show me you are Bronson's daughter, through and through."

I laughed, breathing a sigh of relief. "I choose to take that as a compliment."

"Tell Bronson I said hello."

"I will. Are you sure you can't come?"

"We finally have tickets to see that new Alvin Ailey production at the Fox Theater. We're talking all the grand babies. It took us too long to get them to cancel."

"I hear you. It took Tony months to get them when we went."

And then we ended up not going because he had a last-minute meeting with a client. I took Steena, and we had a ball.

I left the executive suite and headed out to my car. I was going to head home, change and drop by Tony's office on the way to the restaurant. I could still arrive in time to dish with Steena about today's meeting.

And about those damn flowers. But first, I needed to confirm they were not from Tony.

I showered, moisturized, and slipped into a black, knee-length contrast mesh dress and black matte leather heels. I stopped to admire myself in the full-length mirror in my closet, fingering my short curly cut just so, checking the perfect blush application across razor sharp cheekbones and the deep purple Fenty on my lips.

Undefeated was the name of the shade. And the woman, if I had to say so myself.

The dress was clingy, stretching across my full hips, accentuating all my curves, front, back, side. Steena would be amused. My father would grumble about how CEOs— woman CEOs in particular — should dress. His wife would tap his arm and tell him to hush, that I was an adult, and he couldn't tell me what to do anymore.

Especially since I wasn't his employee anymore. That thought made me giggle out loud.

"India Parker. President and Chief Executive Officer," I recited to myself, as I'd done nearly every time I left my condo. Tonight, it was more for reassurance than being a braggart or to pat myself on the back.

Satisfied, I picked up my clutch and keys and left my condo. I rode the elevator back down to my car and I drove the few blocks through traffic to One Atlantic Tower, where several mid-size boutique law firms had established offices.

As an IP attorney, Tony worked with brands to protect their assets and image. One day he could be filing a trademark infringement lawsuit, another day he could be pulling an all-nigher to get a software agreement bent draft completed. Dating Tony meant there would be days I wouldn't see him, calls would go unanswered and dates would be canceled.

And that was, honestly, just fine.

The flowers threw me for a loop, though. If Tony was trying to tell me something, I wanted to put everything on the table so I could decide if I wanted to move forward.

Or step back.

I breezed through the doors to the office suite at Strategic IP Law, LLP. The receptionist was gone for the night, but I knew where I was going. I'd spent a lot of time at Tony's office.

And... on Tony's desk, after hours. A woman didn't need to be in love to have an orgasm. Sometimes Tony got the job done.

The door to his office was closed. I heard noises inside, so I tapped lightly.

"Yeah..." I heard, so I pushed the door open. I'd just stick my head in to ask him to take a break so I could head to dinner. When I opened the door, though...

Well, he *was* in a meeting. Of sorts.

"Oh, yeah... that's it...yeah..."

A caramel toned woman with bottle blonde curly hair was bent over the desk, legs wide, gripping the edge so hard her knuckles were pale. Her skirt was bunched around her waist. A pile of lace sat in the middle of the desk. He'd either taken them off (he loved ripping off a pair of thongs) or she had presented them to him.

Tony's muscled ass cheeks clenched as he thrust his hips in a steady rhythm. His pants were down, pooling at his ankles over his shiny Cole Haan shoes. He didn't even take his boxers off; he pulled them down just far enough to get his dick out. The sounds of sex, tinted by muted grunts and moans, accented by the occasional slap of skin on skin filled the air.

"So I guess you didn't send me the flowers I got today?" I asked, throwing the door open wide.

I almost laughed at the high-pitched shriek that met my ears when the woman he had bent over his desk whipped around to see me standing in the open door, then scrambled away from him while pulling at her skirt.

"Shit!" Tony yelped. He had the good sense to stuff himself back into his boxers and pull up his pants. "I thought you had dinner plans. I told you I—"

"You said you had a deposition. You did not tell me you had a pussy appointment."

"Dammit, India...what the hell are you doing here?"

"Watch your tone. I don't even feel like you can ask me questions right now, but you can tell me who this lovely young lady is," I said, pointing at the woman who looked like she wanted to disappear into a hole in the ground. "Are you an assistant? A junior attorney? Someone Tony is mentoring? This is a hell of a way to get in with a partner track attorney."

"Oh hell nah," she muttered. "You said you was single, you dick!" She grabbed her panties and ran past me.

I snickered. "Does she not read the paper? We're in it every other week."

"Babe. Come on." Tony tucked his shirt into his pants, then zipped them. He was still erect, though I didn't foresee that lasting long. "Look, I've been meaning to talk to you, anyway."

"About her?" I thumbed toward the door. "I hope you've been tested. If you gave me something, I will end you. You know I have the contacts to do it."

"We're not exclusive."

"We're still supposed to be open with each other, so there's no chance of giving each other random shit. You didn't even use a condom. How long have you been sleeping with her?"

"It doesn't matter. We both tested negative. I wouldn't put my career and yours in jeopardy."

"When's the last time you tested?"

"Uh..." He shrugged. "A couple of weeks ago, I guess."

"You guess." I cringed as I made a note to set an appointment with my gynecologist.

"Why are you here? And can you close my door, please?"

Tony looked pathetic. Embarrassed, even. I didn't really care.

"No. It stinks like the sweaty sex you had while you miss your girlfriend's very important dinner to have a quick fuck at work, then wash your dick in the sink before you crawl into her bed later. I'm here because I need to know something. Did you send me flowers today?"

"Flowers?" He scoffed. "I don't do flowers." Tony's face morphed from disgust to suspicion. "Wait... what kind of flowers?"

"Lilies," I replied. Bragged a little. "A dozen. They're gorgeous."

His eyes narrowed to the thinnest of slits in his face. "Who sent you a dozen lilies, India?"

I laughed in his face. "You're jealous right now? Really?"

"A dozen of your favorite flower is a romantic gesture. Who are you messing with?"

"Oh, you know what my favorite flower is. So the half dead roses you pick up from the grocery store are a choice, then. Give me the key to my condo," I demanded. "I'll pack your things and leave them outside my door. Come get them tomorrow, or I'm throwing them out."

He looked like he thought about arguing but saw my expression and gave up. He pulled open a drawer, retrieving his key ring. "We can't talk about this? You want to tie me down and never progress. Forever?"

"Talk about what? You've already decided you want more than me. Or... not me." I nodded toward the open door to indicate the woman that just scurried from his office. "I only really care that you've been lying to me for no reason. You don't have a deposition, do you?"

He exhaled, balanced his elbows on his desk, and clasped his hands. "No."

"No. So we're not at New York Prime sucking down overpriced martinis because... why?"

"Because I don't want to go to dinner with your family and friends."

"So why not be a grown ass man and say that? Why lie and sneak around?"

"Because it would turn into a fight, and I'm tired of pretending we have something worth fighting for. I'm window dressing and arm candy, the occasional steak dinner followed by the weakest blow job I've ever had, and you taking forever to come when we fuck."

I laughed with my mouth wide open, not caring who could hear me. I almost had to take a seat. "Really, Tony? That's where we're going?"

"India—"

"Oh, no. You opened the door, so let's go there, shall we? Because we can talk about how you don't have rhythm unless there's music on. Or we can talk about how you can't get hard without a blue pill and a half hour of lead time. Oh, and a four-hour erection? Where? Because you don't stay hard either."

"Alright, India. That's en—"

"Oh, but wait! There's more! We have yet to talk about how you must be projecting about weak head, because I have faked my *last* orgasm with you. Maybe I'm just giving what I get because I have never had a complaint about my skills. Should I continue? Because I can go all night, unlike you."

He halted me with a hand. "Look, India. Bronson was going to pull me aside this year, like he did last year and the year before, and give me the speech about proposing, making a good woman out of you, how he and Junie are looking forward to us giving him grandchildren. You and I know that isn't happening. Not with me."

I rolled my eyes. "For sure, not with you."

He looked away, stroking his beard. He did that when he was frustrated, pulling at the hairs that needed to be trimmed. If Bronson Parker was anything, he was consistent. I just always thought Tony could handle him.

"Our agreement was convenient, and it served its purpose, but it was never meant to go beyond a year. It's childish. I'm moving up here at the firm. I've got patent work flowing through now, and I'm coming up on forty in a few years. It's time for me to make family moves, and I'm not trying to be nasty, but you're not getting any younger. If you want kids, you need to find somebody to have them with. So I want more. Or I want out."

"Please. Making family moves equates to fucking a woman that works in your office? What if she got caught by someone that wasn't me? Were you going to protect her?"

"She knows what she's doing and so do I. This wasn't our first rodeo."

"Oh...oh. Okay." I'd had enough. I was completely done, thank goodness and good riddance. "My key. Now."

He wrenched the brushed silver key from the ring and handed it to me. "I'm not the enemy, India. I care about you. I just don't want to be your fake boyfriend anymore."

"You *don't* care. You want to fuck people that aren't me

and keep me in the cut for clout. And because of that, you aren't my fake boyfriend anymore."

I tucked the key into my bag and zipped it away, then headed to the door. "By the way… " I asked, turning back to him. "Those Alvin Ailey tickets you got? You didn't have a last-minute client meeting, did you?"

"No," he admitted, scrubbing his hands down his face. "I knew you were dying to see it. I wasn't in the mood for that. I'm more an Anthony Hamilton type of guy. I figured you and Steena would have a better time and I would be free to do… whatever."

"Whatever, indeed."

"So I don't have to go to Bronson's birthday party, then?"

I snickered. I could just imagine Tony calling the day before my father's annual birthday blowout to tell me he would not make it. He'd barely made it the year before.

"Like you were going to actually show up. I think that's a no. And listen…"

His head popped up. The sheen over his eyes and the bags under them said he was tired… but if I wasn't mistaken, he was also relieved. I would be too if I knew I never had to face Bronson Parker again.

"I say this knowing I'm a hypocrite, but stop fucking people at the office. Especially if you're not going to lock the door. It's not even seven o'clock. Anybody could walk up in here."

"Goodbye, India," I heard him reply as I left his office.

Well. I would have some news for Steena at dinner.

I had hoped to get some time alone with Steena at the bar before anyone showed up for dinner, but the newly retired Bronson Parker arrived alongside his wife in a suit and tie, his deep walnut skin glowing against a well-groomed silver beard. Since he now had nothing else to do with his time, he thought he would grab a drink and mingle before our dinner reservations.

So instead of regaling my best friend with the afternoon's developments, I was entertaining my father and Junie.

While I had a relationship with my mother, she and my father divorced when I was young. They shared custody and my brothers and I bounced back and forth between houses while she pursued the career of her dreams. Now she was a jet-setting marketing executive and would have attended my dinner were she not in Europe crafting a global launch for a new sneaker brand. My father remarried after many years of friendship with a woman from his social club. Junie has always been… just Junie. She, in no way, wanted to play or replace our mother.

"So, how was the annual planning session?" Dad asked, over the din of conversation and the waitstaff placing glasses, silverware, and plates. He held the first of many whiskey sours, I was sure, in one hand. "That was today, wasn't it?"

"It was today. And it went… alright." I shrugged, then deflected by sucking down a swallow of the pink martini in front of me.

"Bronson, you would have been so proud of your baby girl! They showed up with attitude, but she told them folks what was what."

I glared at Steena out of the corner of my eye. I had opted not to tattle on the team. Not yet anyway.

"As I told you I'd have to do, I made it clear who runs the show. I don't think we will have any further issue and if we do, I'm ready to handle it. I just hope I didn't come off like I was pulling rank and about to tell my daddy on them."

"They forced your hand, and it needed to be said," Steena replied.

My brain was second-guessing and editing that unrehearsed speech over and over. I probably could have found a better way to make my point, but... why should I have had to? They'd never tell a man to mince his words and be nice.

"Was Evelyn there?" Asked Dad. "What did she say?"

"She... "I smiled, trying not to laugh. "She said I was Bronson Parker's daughter, through and through."

He let out a long, loud gust of laughter. "Yep," he said, when he caught his breath. "You know you're on the right path when Evelyn goes to bat for you. She's your secret weapon."

I took that note to heart. "Some of them have been with Parker for a long time. They don't want the business to fail and I'm sympathetic to that."

"And it won't."

"They also think they're the ones that have been keeping Parker afloat since you left the day-to-day business."

He coughed an impatient huff. "I turned over a company in good standing to a highly capable executive. What in hell did they think we were doing for the last three years?"

"I'm not sure, Dad. But they won't deter me from my mission."

"They certainly will not," Dad confirmed, offering his whiskey in toast. He stretched his lips into a tight grin. "You promised me something new in the coming year, something bigger than the service kiosks. I'm eager to see what you come up with."

"Honestly, so am I, Dad."

My evening bag vibrated in my lap, alerting me to a new message on my phone. Since I took over Parker, the after-hours contact had mostly ceased. Those calls and emails now went to Steena. The only people that would reach out to me after work hours now were Evelyn— who was enjoying a show at the Fox Theater with her husband and grandchildren— and Steena, seated next to me.

I slid away my drink and pulled the device from my bag to peek at the screen. For a moment, I wasn't sure I'd seen what I saw. So I looked again.

To: India.Parker@ParkerEnt.com
From: Malik@HinesTech.com
Subject: Flowers

Hi.

I hope I don't have to reintroduce myself, but if I do, I deserve it. I wanted to make sure you got the flowers. I hope you still like lilies.

It's been a pleasure to watch you rise. Congratulations on a great year. Hope you see so many more.

Yours,
Malik

My *ex-boyfriend* Malik Hines.

Pecan toned, hazel eyed, voice as smooth as a top shelf liquor and just as brown, super techy, *good with his hands...*Malik Hines.

The same Malik Hines that I hadn't seen in years had just confirmed that he sent that gorgeous bouquet.

I knew it. It had to be Malik.

I locked the phone and glanced around the table. My brothers and their wives, a few family friends and business associates were laughing, drinking and chatting like my life was not slowly flipping upside down.

First Tony fucks everything all the way up.

Then the man I had to train myself out of longing for leaps into main character position.

What the fuck is happening?

My backup plan was to drag Steena for drinks after dinner to tell her about Tony's shenanigans, but I needed to talk to her.

Now.

I pointed to my phone, interrupting a story Steena started to tell my parents. "Sorry. Quick work issue we need to deal with. Step out with me?"

"Work issue? This time of night?" My father asked, looking up from a steaming bowl of She-Crab soup. "They shouldn't be calling you away from the dinner table."

"It's nothing big, Dad. Just something that would be easier if Steena and I stepped away. One call and it'll be settled. We'll be right back."

I pushed my chair back from the table and nodded at Steena. She placed her napkin next to her plate and stood.

"I don't understand—"

"You aren't supposed to understand," interrupted Junie.

Her countenance and the edge to her voice said her patience was waning thin. "You're retired. Eat your soup and enjoy not having to know."

I winked at her and whisked Steena away toward the restrooms, pausing in a dimly lit hallway once we were far enough away from the dining room.

"India, what is happening?" She muttered, her thumb gliding across the screen of her phone. "I don't have any new email, and I know the staff would email me before you."

I waved her phone away. "I had to get you away from the table because this can't wait. So. Guess what I walked in on when I went to see Tony."

"Uh..." She shook her head, her brows forming a V between her eyes. "Didn't he have a deposition?"

"Oh, he had a deposition, alright." I leaned in to mutter, "A deposition of his dick into some pussy that ain't mine."

Steena gasped, jumping back, then slapped a hand over her mouth, eyes wide. "Oh. My. Lord," I heard, from behind her hand. "In the office? Just... in the office?"

"In the office. Bent over the desk with the door unlocked."

"Oh..." She removed her hand, then blanked her expression. "To be fair, you've been in the same position, India."

"Not during the damn day, Steena! It wasn't even seven o'clock."

"True. What did Anthonius have to say for himself?"

I rolled my eyes, sucking my teeth. "Some bullshit about being tired of playing my pretend boyfriend. He wants something serious, but I'm holding us up... blah blah, whatever."

"Well, it *has* been three years. So he's fucking other

people? That... that's his way of saying he wanted more with you?"

"I told him to take the out, 'cause his ass has been lying for a long time. He's not here tonight because he didn't want to have the same talk my dad gives him every year about us getting married and giving him grandchildren."

"Did you ask him about the flowers? He sent them, right?"

"He said, and I quote, *I don't do flowers.*"

"He *didn't* send you the flowers." I felt a satisfied smile bend my lips. "That shit-eating grin tells me you know who did, though."

"You know who did, too! Look what I just got in my inbox."

I held the phone up so she could see. Steena grabbed the phone and scrolled, then enlarged the screen. Then, slowly, her gaze lifted from the phone to my eyes.

"Ooh, girl."

My head bobbed one deep, resolute nod. "I knew it. Something told me."

"Something like him being the only man that ever sent you those kind of flowers? Genius."

"Your ass tried to tell me it was Tony!"

"Because I didn't want Malik's trifling ass to make his way back into your life. Where the hell did he come from? It's been years!"

I took the phone from her, locking it again. "Tony had the nerve to act jealous once he realized somebody sent me that big ass vase of flowers."

Steena cringed. "With his dick still wet from the chick he's screwing instead of you? The nerve. Please tell me he exists in the past tense."

"I made him give me my key. We're done."

I rolled my eyes up to meet hers and menacingly rubbed my palms together. "I think this could be a sign—"

"It's not," she snapped, leaning in. "It's not a sign of anything."

"Steena—"

"India! If anything, it's a sign to ignore a man that walked away from a very good thing for no damn reason and hasn't spoken to you since. You spent a good two years of prime time pining for ol' boy. You are in a good spot right now, and you just got rid of some heavy baggage in the shape of a man named *Anthonius.* Now is not the time for you to be weak, India."

"I am hardly weak, Kristeena."

"I see it in your eyes," she retorted, leaning in. "He is nothing but trouble, and you know it. Don't do it. Reconsider."

"Hear me out. We could just talk. You said yourself, it's been years. We could catch up—"

"You know good and well that catching up is not what's on your mind right now."

"Are you even listening to me?"

"I'm not." She shook her head, curls bouncing. "I'm not. And it's going both ways, cause you don't hear me, neither."

She tossed up her hands and flounced away but came back.

"You're gonna do what you wanna do, so I don't even know why you're bringing this up to me, but let me remind you that a woman in your position cannot afford to be caught up with some random man. You have eyes on you. You can't sneeze without an article popping up in the Business Chronicle."

I snorted. It was light and ladylike, but I definitely

snorted. "I'm not worried about the Chronicle. And Malik is not a random man. I know him. Intimately."

"You don't need to remind me. I don't want to pick your heart up off the street again. It doesn't matter how casual you and Tony were. You walked in your man inside some other woman. You're officially on the rebound. Weak. Vulnerable. Prone to flesh-led decisions."

She was right, though I hated to admit it. The sudden appearance of his name in my inbox spurred an instant obsession with a man I thought I'd spend my life with not so long ago. My thoughts were already consumed by the chance of a reconnection, and not just to chat about old times. I'd been putting up with Tony's lack of bedroom prowess for so long that I almost forgot what it was like to be satisfied in bed.

And if I remembered anything about Malik, it was that he studied what brought me pleasure and never failed to bring to me to the brink... and then push me over the cliff. I was already throbbing and entertaining wild daydreams about a reconnection.

I couldn't stop wanting it... as soon as fucking possible.

"Steen." I placed my hands on her shoulders and gave her a firm, loving squeeze. "My dearest friend. I love you, I hear you, I *am* listening, even though you feel like I'm not. But like you said, I'm going to do what I want to do. I can hide it from you or I can share it with you. Pick your battle."

"Do not even *think* about hiding shit from me!" Steena's whisper was hoarse and not all that quiet.

"That's what I thought you'd say."

"So, what are you going to do? You don't even know if this man is still in Atlanta."

"I don't know yet. I'll figure it out."

"Well, when you know, fill a sister in, but we need to get back to dinner before Bronson sends out a search party."

"You know you love me," I joked, leading us back down the hall to the table.

"That doesn't mean I'm not tired of your ass. Please tell me you're actually working out of your new office tomorrow, Ms. CEO."

"I think Evelyn will call security if I don't. IT is moving all my equipment tomorrow. And the interior designers will be in next week, thank God."

We slipped back into our seats and spread napkins across our laps.

"Redecorating?" Asked Junie. "It's about time. Bronson's office looks like a Billy Dee Williams ad for Colt 45."

"It does not," my father protested. "It was classy, in its day."

"Its day was 1972, Dad."

"It works every time..." said Steena, reciting the popular ad copy. While the table laughed about malt liquor and old alcohol ads, I opened the mail app and tapped out a quick reply.

To: Malik@HinesTech.com
From: India.Parker@ParkerEnt.com
Subject: Re: Flowers

Malik,

I received the flowers! I didn't know who to thank, so I appreciate you reaching out. They're beautiful, and I'm touched that you remembered my favorite.

It's been a very long time, and I would love to catch up.

In person. Very soon.

India

I hit 'send' before I could change my mind.

"Everything okay?" Dad asked, his tone low, deep lines of concern across his forehead.

"Of course, Dad," I answered, beaming a reassuring smile in his direction. I picked up a spoon and stirred a cooling bowl of soup. "There should be no further interruption. Did you decide what you're ordering for your entrée?"

CHAPTER FIVE

Full of soup, salad, steak and potatoes from New York Prime, one of Atlanta's finest steakhouses, I picked up my car from the valet and pointed it toward home, just a few minutes away from the restaurant.

The luxury vehicle glided smoothly along the city streets, wet and shiny from recent rain. I turned the stereo to LL Cool J's *Rock the Bells* Sirius XM station and nodded my head to an old-school hip-hop classic. I'd been hoping to hear one of my favorite songs, a blast from the past that had good memories attached to it, but it never played when I wanted it to play.

It didn't matter. I had the album on vinyl and CD and, as soon as I got home, I kicked off my shoes and headed to the stereo system in the living room. I picked through my collection until I found the one I was looking for.

LL Cool J, Mr. Smith.

Steena rolled her eyes at my collection and insistence on buying CDs and records instead of using a streaming service. The sound was just... *better*. I didn't spend good money on surround sound in the car and in my home, with speakers piped into every room to hear downgraded qual-ity. Especially not my favorites.

Especially not *this song*.

I hummed through the opening strains, the soft tap of the drum, the intro vocals of *Hey Lover*. I picked up my shoes, carrying them into my bedroom and tucked them into their slot in the walk-in closet, enjoying the full sound of a romantic, rhythmic ode to a lover throughout my apartment.

I pulled off my evening wear, dumping assorted items into baskets-lingerie, laundry, and dry cleaning. Then I stepped into the adjoining bathroom for a long, luxurious shower while the rest of the album played and memories rolled in like a thick fog.

Malik and I met at Emory University as advisors to first-year students in the residence halls and often planned events and programming together. He was cute...and didn't seem to know it. My younger residents wasted a lot of time flirting with him, but he was hyper focused on his courses and extra-curricular activities, namely a group he called Code Club, which was a group of guys in his computer programming classes that liked to write programs for fun.

Malik was brilliant in a way that I found inspiring and so comfortable in his geek era. I found that wildly sexy. He was also hilariously dry, particularly when it came to the type of guys I went out with. He never liked anyone I dated.

"That dude whack," he'd comment when I told him I had a date.

"You say that about every guy I go out with."

"I know. Cause they're all whack."

"Stop saying that. So I have bad taste?"

"No. It has nothing to do with you. They're not good enough for you."

"What, like I'm too good for somebody?"

"I didn't say that. I said they're not good enough for *you*. There's a difference. But go 'head," he'd say with a shrug of his shoulders. "Have fun. Call me when you get home."

I admitted to eventually just trying to find a man that he would approve of.

It never happened.

After graduation, I went straight to grad school. Malik wrote programs for a health care company and toiled after hours to set up his tech company. He talked nonstop about his vision for games specifically written for and marketed to Black gamers.

While I lived at home, my father and Junie traveled often, and when my parents were away, Malik would come over, hang out, eat, study. He was very much living the young, hungry professional life, and I liked making sure he got at least one good meal.

Malik and I lounged on a Friday night in the basement den in front of a wide, theater-style TV. I'd been studying for an exam and he was writing the same game he'd been talking about since undergrad, about brothers having adventures in space. A break from work and study turned into Malik picking through my CD collection, then finding LL Cool J's Mr. Smith album and breaking down every song, every lyric, every riff, every beat.

"This is my favorite song," I swooned, while *Hey Lover* soared through the speakers.

"I like it too. It, uh...it holds a lot of meaning for me." We were a few glasses of wine and most of a pizza deep into conversation. The room was warm, the conversation loose, so his sudden dive into a quiet, meaningful tone was a swerve. "I mean, like... he's talking for me. About me, how I feel about a person. You know what I'm saying?"

I gasped, scooting over on the couch. "Malik! Do you have a crush I don't know about? Tell me!"

"Yeah, actually. You might know her. Real well."

"Oh." I swallowed hard, realizing all at once what he meant. "Well, if it's Steena, you'll have to compete with Method Man."

He laughed, but his shoulders dropped. The anticipation of the moment, the space between us, the weight of what he was trying to say was... so much. We needed that levity.

"Steena is great. I like her a lot...but it's not her."

My heart skipped a beat, and my breath hitched in my throat. I wasn't expecting a vulnerable moment, but now that it was here...I'd been hoping for it.

"Okay. So it seems we have a lot to talk about, suddenly."

"Yeah. But not really suddenly, is it? I've spent a lot of time watching you date a lot of guys that..." He shook his head. "It took me a while to realize why I couldn't get with the idea of you being with someone. By the time I could be honest with myself, my feelings were full-blown. We're adults with jobs and responsibilities and this— how I feel about you... it's more than fleeting thoughts and nervous butterflies and daydreaming. It's way more than a crush by now."

"We have known each other for a long time, Malik. *Years.* You're just now sitting on my couch letting LL Cool J tell me how you feel about me?"

"How I have *felt* about you," he corrected. "I have had this urge to tell you how I feel for a long ass time. More than that? I think the feeling is mutual."

"Oh, you do?" I leaned back, brows high. "Uh… what makes you think that, Mr. Hines?"

"No need to get formal, Ms. Parker," he shot back, laughing. "I'm the same dude I was at Emory when we planned events for our floors together. When you came to the little graduation party my dad threw at West End Pizza. When you made sure I got an invite to the classy soiree your parents planned for you. And…"

He paused, hunching his shoulders, waving a hand around the room. "It is Friday night. Prime time. Date night. You could be anywhere with anybody, but you made sure I knew I was invited over here to spend time with you."

"I have an exam on Monday, and you work better when I keep you on task and make you take breaks, so yeah. I invited you over."

"You can pretend it's casual and a friendship thing, but I know you. I mean something to you, India. We have something real and special, and I don't have much, but I'm betting what I've got that it's more than friendship."

My heart pounded so hard I could barely hear the words. I felt them, though. Every sound, every syllable. I cleared my throat. Then scooted closer.

"Maybe… maybe you're not all the way wrong."

"I'm not?"

I cackled. "You sounded so sure five seconds ago. Now I have to confirm?"

"Just for clarity, yeah. Because I could be off. I don't think I am but, yes. I'd like you to confirm there's more here between us than two old friends hanging out."

There was something about the soft grit in his voice and the unguarded desire in his eyes that made my head bob, confirming what we both knew. There was something between us, and it was certainly more than an immature, surface-level crush.

His gaze shot up to meet mine. In a swift moment, every ounce of attraction beamed from him to me. Instead of suppressing it like I had been, a steady tendril of desire smoldered. Malik reached to grab my hand, placing it on his chest. His heart thumped hard beneath my palm.

I answered the question his eyes were asking. "Yeah, you're right. The feeling is actually very mutual."

In a fraction of a moment, he covered my mouth with his. Then he moved closer, his body a solid wall of heat that crushed my chest as though he couldn't get close enough. His mouth devoured mine, ramping up the flames between us. I was more than ready to be consumed by him. But just as a low moan of ecstasy escaped, he pulled back.

"I... I want to. But we can't, not in your parent's house."

Disappointed, but knowing he was right, I scooted back. "I know. I wish you would have made that move a long time ago."

"I've wanted to," he said. "That can't be a surprise to you."

"No," I replied, leaning in again. "It's not."

Whenever he emailed, texted, left me a note, his messages began with *Hey Lover.* For years, I longed to open an email or a text message and see those words again.

I finished my shower, body oil rub down and evening routine, then pulled on a gray cotton t-shirt that fell to mid-thigh. I grabbed my phone from my purse, and padded barefoot to the kitchen, frowning when I bent to look into the wine fridge to see that I was out of my favorite wine.

"Ugh."

IndiaJParker: Who has two thumbs and forgot to re-up on Stella Rosa? This girl. Brilliant.

I closed the twitter app and wandered back to my bedroom, where I pulled back the heavy duvet and slid between cool, high thread count sheets.

My phone chimed the tone I assigned to Steena.

> Steena: Hey girl. Checking in. Do I need to make an emergency wine run over there?

I chuckled.

> India: Stop stalking my tweets. I'm okay. I guess. You want to go for drinks on Saturday?

> Steena: Saturday? Not tomorrow? Keeping our options open, are we?

> India: Whatever, Steen. I am in the bed.

> Steena: I'll let you know about Saturday. Might have an option.

> India: Tramp, you haven't told me about any options. Who you hiding from me?

> Steena: Nothing worth hiding is happening over here, but I'll fill you in if things escalate.

> Steena: And don't change the subject. Be careful, young lady. You have a lot more to lose than he does.

> India: Love you. See you in the morning.

Steena: Love you back.

It was one thing to joke about reaching out to Malik. But after dinner and drinks, and breaking off a three-year relationship, even if it was fake, the realities of the life I lived smacked me in the face.

I was lying in a bed where the other side would stay cold for the foreseeable future, staring at the ceiling and recreating the love scenes, the highlights, the best parts that never left my mind. And preparing myself for the heartache that could come from rekindling an old flame that was maybe never meant to burn again.

Statistics show that men who walk away almost always try to come back. I didn't think it would take as long as it did. I also didn't think he would cut me off— move out of his apartment, change his phone number, dead his email address.

But I knew I would know Malik Hines again. That we would reconnect on his terms.

My phone vibrated a new email notification. I scrolled past Instagram, Facebook and Twitter messages from well-wishers who wanted to send me wine.

To: India.Parker@ParkerEnt.com

From: Malik@Hinestech.com

Subject: Re: Re: Flowers

I agree that it's been way too long, and that's my fault. Love that you liked the flowers. I still got it.;)

You said you wanted to catch up. In person. *Very* soon.

I take your words to heart. If you're serious, say less.

I'm up and unless you've moved, I remember where you live.

If it's too late for a visit, slide me a phone number. We could FaceTime.

Malik

Whew, shit.

The way the tone of his email made me smile and warmth bloom in my belly was... dangerous. Did this man just offer to come to my place? At... I checked the time on my iPad—10 PM?

"Boy," I whispered, my fingers immediately flying across the screen, "If you don't stop fucking playing with me."

CHAPTER SIX

THE STUDIO WAS QUIET. NOT EMPTY, SINCE ONE DEVELOPER SPENT overnight hours correcting code.

Corey sat hunched over his keyboard at his custom workstation, headphones over his ears and fingers moving from keyboard to mouse and back again. He was in his own world, surrounded by monitors. Occasionally, his head would pop up to check one. If his fix worked, he'd grunt, silently fist bump himself, then duck back down into his man-made fortress.

I was beat from a long day of staring at computer screens, but also wired because I'd emailed India back with a bold, braggadocios offer. I picked up on *in person* and *very soon* and boy-bossed too close to the sun. I expected her to laugh off the suggestion and counter with a more appropriate time and place.

She'd called my bluff.

To: Malik@HinesTech.com
From: IndiaParker@gmail.com

Subject: new email address

I don't know about you, but I can't flirt with my
ex over corporate email. Use this address.
I'm up… but you knew I would be. I want to see
you. I want to hug your neck and hear your voice.
If you feel comfortable, come through.
India

I read her note over again, knowing the appropriate response should be a warm acknowledgment of how long it had been since we shared the same space, but also that it would not be the best idea for me to drive the nineteen minutes (according to Google maps) from my studio to her mid-city condo.

I was not a fool, though. I was not about to decline. I wanted to get into my car and race toward her. I wanted to hope there would be more to this invite than chatting it up about the good old days.

I wanted to hope for reconciliation, even if I didn't deserve it, even if it was only the friendship that could be salvaged after all this time. Even if we were still socially and financially uneven, for an inelegant way to put it, it didn't matter so much anymore.

I didn't deserve her forgiveness or her kindness or her kisses or her body, after I walked out on her the way I did. I had to figure, though… even if she invited me over to curse me out and gain the closure she should have had seven years ago, it would mean seeing her again. Sharing the same air and space in a room.

I would take it.

I rolled my wrist to check my watch. 10:09 PM

beamed up at me. If I still knew her as well as I used to, she was a night owl that didn't require more than a few hours of sleep. India would be awake until at least midnight.

"Damn! You scared the shit outta me, man. What are you doing?"

I almost dropped the phone as I turned to find Corey behind me in the kitchen doorway. His sweatshirt had the Morehouse Computer Labs logo screen-printed across the chest. He looped his headphones around his neck and stared, eyes open wide.

"Corey..." I had overfilled my cup, then spilled half its contents when I whipped around. "What are *you* doing?"

"I saw a shadow and thought I heard something. I came to check things out. Come to find out it's just you creepin' around here."

I shoved the phone in my pocket and grabbed a handful of napkins to sop up the water. Corey grabbed a mop from the pantry and cleaned behind me while I chased water around the kitchen.

"Yo, Malik," he said, returning the mop to the pantry when he finished. "You good?"

"Yeah. Sorry, I didn't mean to scare you. You were in the zone over there at your station. I just needed some water, and I got distracted."

He squinted, humming a little. "I mean overall. You been like... here, but not. You don't really sleep."

"You would know, since you don't either," I quipped, tossing the napkins in the recycling bin. Rebekah would have a fit if she saw paper in the garbage in the morning.

"I sleep. These are prime hours for me. That's why I like that Brandon gives me the overnight fixes. I get tired around 4 AM, knock out for a few hours, then head to class.

You pace all night. And then pace all day. So I'm just checking in."

"Thanks for checking in. I'm good," I replied, summoning up a smile. "Just got a lot on my mind. I'm not gonna get too many chances to make a first impression. GameBox is a big deal, and we need to be ready. I want it to be...."

I pondered my next few words. "Galaxy Bros needs to be worth the wait."

Corey's head bobbed, the edges of his mouth pulling down. "Respect. I'm about to grab some caffeine and get back to work, then."

"Appreciate that. I'm uh..." My pocket buzzed, so I pulled out my phone. India had tweeted.

IndiaJParker: Who has two thumbs and forgot to re-up on Stella Rosa? This girl. Brilliant.

My breath caught in my throat. I physically made myself push it out, then tucked my bottom lip between my teeth.

"I uh... I need to run out for a minute. A friend needs... a friend needs me. You'll be fine by yourself?"

"I'm an adult, Malik," said Corey. He pulled a few cans of soda from the refrigerator and headed back to his workstation.

I took the stairs two at a time to my living quarters. The landing was outfitted with a flat screen TV, a leather two-seater couch and my father's old La-Z-Boy lounger led to my bedroom and private bathroom. My loft was simple but comfortable, an upstairs corner of the warehouse space. It was initially meant for storage, but the previous tenant had renovated the area with plumbing, fixtures, and a door for a private office, so I repurposed it.

I rifled through my drawers, finally picking out a pair of sweatpants and pulling them on. I changed into the first clean t-shirt I could get my hands on, then zipped a hoodie over it. I glanced at my hair and face on the way out, but I was stepping out post shower routine, so I wasn't looking too crazy. I pushed my wallet into one pocket and grabbed my keys.

And my phone. With a thumb, I punched out *on the way*.

Right after I made a stop at the liquor store for wine. Couldn't show up empty-handed.

"Later, Corey. If you leave, lock up," I called on my way out.

My trusty Toyota, which had carried me through the leanest of times, was cold since it had been sitting in the rain, then the cooling night air. It started right up though, and as if it were seven years earlier and I was on automatic, I pointed the car toward India's place.

I was trying not to hope, but I could almost feel her fold into my arms and mold her body to mine. I wanted to be reminded of the soft, supple landscape of her skin, the signature scent that clung to her clothing and brought her to mind long after I left her.

Which, I hoped, wouldn't happen for a few hours.

CHAPTER SEVEN

India: In the interest of not keeping things from you… I may come in late tomorrow.

The FaceTime notification rang out and Steena's face popped up on my phone.

"Relax, fun police." I cackled as I picked up, then scooted back on the bed and sank against a mountain of pillows. "I'm alone. You're not slick, by the way. Facetiming me instead of calling."

Steena heaved an obviously exasperated breath. I loved getting her all worked up. She was barefaced, her brown skin dewy fresh. She wore a festive pair of pajamas and was seated at the vanity in her well-lit bathroom. Her hair was halfway wrapped, so she was on her way to bed.

"I knew he wasn't over there," she said, pointing at the camera with her paddle brush. "But I can tell you got something going on. He's on the way over there, isn't he?"

I glanced at the tablet on my nightstand, where a duplicate of my personal email account was on display. *On my way,* he'd sent just minutes ago.

"Maybe."

"India Parker…"

"Fine, since you know so much! Yes, he is on the way, and before you butt in… *I know*. My eyes are wide open. I know exactly what he is coming over here for and if he wants it, he can get it. Tony had sex today, and I didn't. And that ain't right."

"You're not keeping score with Anthonius."

"I deserve to feel good after today. Tell me I'm wrong for thinking that."

"Nope. Not wrong at all."

"Okay, so that's what's happening, and I wanted you to know what was up."

"Thanks for the scoop, but honey…" She pushed a hard breath from her lungs as she resumed wrapping her hair, pushing the silky press around her head with the brush. "Did you look him up at all? What do the Googles say?"

"Do I have to remind you that I am intimately acquainted with Malik? I don't need to look him up."

She lowered the brush again and stared directly into the camera. Right through my damn soul. "What if he shows up talking about his wife of five years and their beautiful twin boys? What if he wants to show off his white picket fence and life in the 'burbs and shit?"

"Then my thirsty ass gets what I deserve. But I'll tell you something, Steena," I continued, a sultry smile spreading slowly across my lips. "Malik Hines did not send me a specialty flower arrangement and get in his car after ten o'clock on a Thursday night to come tell me about his wife and children."

She pursed her lips while sliding bobby pins into her hair, then she picked up a scarf and fluttered it out, letting it settle over her hair. "And that's how you're looking? Scarf and sleep shirt? You're gonna make him work, huh?"

"It's not like he's never seen me in a headscarf. And excuse me, this scarf is stylish! Check out my cute bow and everything." I turned my head to the side to show off my skills. "If I still know Malik, it will not faze him one bit."

"And what if you *don't* still know Malik? Hmm? What if this man is a completely different person, seven years later? What if he gets over there and he don't want nothin' but to talk?"

"Then we'll talk! At which point it won't matter that I'm in my scarf. I'm not about to get up and get fine for him. I don't have to impress him; I did all that work already and I'm not going backwards."

"I guess. Now I know you know, but I have to say it. If something jumps off, make sure he wraps it up."

"What do you mean, *if?* My goal for tonight is to make sure something jumps off."

"You are a mess," Steena replied, sucking her teeth. "Be good, girl. Or... be very bad and tell me about it tomorrow."

"Oh, I will," I promised, sending her off with a cheeky grin.

I returned the phone to the charging stand and took a long glance around the room. I got up, re-made the bed, then went to the bureau to pick out a pair of leggings to pull on.

I took a quick turn through the apartment, not only to straighten up but to gather anything that belonged to Tony: his robe hanging in my bathroom, his shower kit and toothbrush, a tube of Rogaine, a container of Just for Men hair dye, some specialty cinnamon raisin bread he liked to keep in my freezer. I dropped everything into an empty box and tossed the few photos I had of him on top, then fit the lid over the box. I doubted he would come by for just a few items but they would be ready if he did. The chances of those items landing in the dumpster behind the building by the weekend were high.

Just as I had set the box next to the front door, I heard the faint sound of the elevator arriving on the floor. This time of night, it could only be Malik making his way down the hall. I peeked quickly in the mirror, tugged at the scarf keeping my edges on point, and tightened the bow. I inhaled a deep breath through my nose and blew it out to quell my nerves.

What if Steena was right?

What if Malik was drastically different from I remembered? What if he was a whole new man?

Then you're about to meet the new Malik Hines.

I reached for the door just as three quick knocks sounded. I sucked in a breath and swung the door open.

My first sighting of him face to face in seven years was breathtaking and weird and nerve-wracking and wonderful... and worth every second I'd had to wait.

Malik Hines darkening my doorway again was all I ever wanted.

He was so casually sexy, like he just hopped up from the couch and rolled on over, but my heart thumped like I was staring at a runway model in a designer suit: zip up hoodie, sweatpants, Nikes with no socks on his feet. His hair and beard were cut close, and he sported a sexy, distinguished salt and pepper mix.

I felt myself boomerang back to this moment seven years ago. All I had now were regrets—the words I could have said to reassure him that I would love him through his lean times, words that would have magically changed his mind and saved our relationship. The stoic decision I'd made to give him the space and time he asked for, because he loved me enough to do the work.

I loved him enough to hope he would reach out when he was ready.

Was he ready?

It must have been the same for Malik because he stood speechless, motionless in my doorway. But then he beamed that smile I remembered, that I could never forget. And when his lips parted, I knew what he was going to say.

"Hey, lover," we greeted each other in unison. And then laughed so hard, so loud, I had to grab his arm and drag him inside before my neighbors complained.

"Here's where I admit to being a creep," he said, holding up a black plastic bag that was weighted down with something. I glanced inside, then grinned at the bottle of Stella Rosa Black.

"You saw my tweet. Thank you because I really wanted some tonight and I'm completely out."

He moved further inside the foyer and my heart did a little dance in my chest. I closed the door behind him and turned to find him... still there. I wasn't dreaming.

"I can't believe I'm looking at you right now. You're really here," I said, openly swooning.

"When India Parker says move..." Malik shrugged, then opened his arms. "Should we... should we hug or...? I don't know what to do with my hands."

"We should definitely hug."

I leaped into his arms, wrapping my limbs around his neck. He lifted me off the ground like I was a feather and held me against his body for longer than I expected, and for far shorter a span of time than I really wanted. I could have hung there forever. It was so... *so* good to be in his arms again.

"Ooh," I swooned, sliding down his body as he slowly released me, then stepped back. "Looking real good, Malik."

"You ain't got to lie," he replied, rubbing a palm over his head with a shy half-smile. "I'm rough tonight. All this salt in my pepper, all this weight I've put on…"

"I ain't got to lie, and I'm not about to start. Trust me, the years have been very kind to you. Take the compliment."

"I'll take it, only because you obviously know what amazing looks like. Definitely wearing the hell out of that scarf and those leggings are doing the Lord's work. You do not miss leg day."

"My trainer is doing the damn thing." I twirled in my foyer, grinning like a fool while he leered with exaggeration. "I could go for a nightcap. How about you? We have so much catching up to do."

"Shoes off, right?" He asked, already toeing off his Nike sneakers. "*You* have catching up to do. I've been following your career. Parker doesn't stay out of the business news too long."

"Don't remind me how much you remember about me."

I led him through the foyer, past the dining room, which was dimly lit by a single lamp and the lights of the Christmas tree. The kitchen was a wide-open space with a view of the living room over the center island.

"You remembered my favorite flower, even where to get them. You seem to remember where I live with no prompting."

"You're not that hard to keep track of," he replied. He pulled the bottle of wine from the bag and removed the foil wrapper. I made no effort to hide my stares at the muscles in his arms as he twisted the cap off. He set the bottle and the cap on the counter.

"Did you want wine?" I offered, pulling two stemless glasses from the cabinet. "Stella is sweet. I have Sauvignon or Chardonnay and I might have some beer leftover from the last time Steena was here. She likes that imported stuff."

He shook his head. "I don't drink anymore, actually. Dad's cancer fight kind of scared me into living healthier. A *little*. I'll take some water, though."

"I wish I could say I had heard what you've been doing. I looked for information on your dad to at least send something to his service, but nobody named Clifford Hines had a service in Atlanta."

I grabbed a bottle of water to hand to him, then poured just enough wine to say I had a drink before sliding on to the couch next to him. It was still so surreal to be in the same room with him. Any second now, I'd pinch myself and wake up in my big, empty bed.

"I appreciate that." He cracked the seal on the bottle of water and opened it, pouring a large gulp down his throat. "There was no service, though," he continued, "because my dad's actually still kicking. Driving me and Brandon crazy."

My mouth fell open in surprise. I was upset that I wouldn't be there to support Malik after the loss of his father.

"But...he was so sick the last time we spoke."

"Yeah. He's our big miracle." He answered, his mouth doing that proud downturn while his head bobbed a nod. "We did chemo, which you know... it hurts while it's helping. It shrank the tumor enough to remove a portion of his colon. That gave us a break to let him get some weight on, get his strength up. He just barely qualified for a drug trial, and that was his ticket to health."

He seemed relieved. Hearing this great news, so was I.

"Well, healthy enough. The drug keeps him stable, and he's careful about his diet. He's been on a low dose of oral chemo and this immunotherapy treatment for some time, but he's holding. The experience opened his eyes, and he decided to start really living."

"So he's...stable? Not in remission."

"Right," I confirmed with a nod. "The meds will work as long as they are going to work and then..." Malik hunched his shoulders. "He doesn't want anything invasive. No more surgery, no IV chemo. He's down in Panama Beach right now, terrorizing every woman over fifty."

I smiled at a warm memory of Cliff. "I remember he used to flirt hard with me and Steena."

"He's still a sucker for a beautiful woman."

"It's great that he's still here. And I'm so happy to hear he's well enough to be a menace. So Brandon is good, too? Did he ever open his shop?" Malik's brother had been obsessed with cars. He loved video games almost as much as he loved cars.

"Yeah, Brandon is great. He has a foreign auto repair and customization spot. And he works with me at Hines Tech, keeping all the programming in line. He loves bossing me around."

"I remember that bossy little high yellow boy."

"Well, now he's a big bossy high yellow boy. Taller than I am. Wider than I am. About to get married."

"That's so good to hear. It's nice to work with family." I bobbed my head, re-thinking that. "Sometimes. You know what I mean."

He laughed, nodding. "Yeah, I do."

"And so..." I sank into the couch, creeping closer to him, so close I could feel the heat radiating from his thighs. "How are *you*, Malik?"

He paused, and his smile faltered. Whether he lost his answer or needed time to ponder the question, the room was quiet and still for a long moment.

"Hey, it's just a question," I lobbed softly. "I'm not trying to catch you in anything. I want to know how you are because I haven't seen you in a while."

"I know," he said, his tone so low it was almost a whisper. "And… I'm sorry about that. I've needed to say I'm sorry for seven years. I've needed to apologize for how things went down between us. I was really hoping you didn't open the door and swing on me."

"You know I'm not a fighter, but there was a time when I would have been tempted. Yes, you did me dirty, blocking me everywhere, moving out of your apartment, changing your number, dumping your email address…"

"Shit," he said, leaning forward and bunching his shoulders up by his ears. He rested his elbows on his knees and let out a low groan. "I forgot about all that. I was lost. Real lost for a while. I had so much bad shit swirling around, and I couldn't handle the thought of disappointing you. I didn't want that to be one more thing not going right so—"

"So you destroyed it on purpose," I finished for him. When he didn't respond, not even to deny it, I pressed. "Was it worth it?"

"Depends on the day," he replied.

He straightened and sat up, as if he needed to face me, head on. Stoic.

"Some days… I don't know how I am. It's a never-ending merry-go-round. I'm the person in charge of everything and everybody. I'm the one carrying the world on my shoulders. Those are the days I wish I didn't push away the one person who was always in my corner, telling me every-thing is going to be alright."

I nodded, feeling what he was saying.

"Most days, though? I know how hard I worked to get here. I know I'm better than I was the last time we saw each other. I think a lot about what my dad says about living while you have life. Don't have regrets. Heal. Make amends. Set things right. I'm different. I guess that's how I am."

"I think different is the best we're going to get. And if it's a good different, then I'm happy for you."

"We both know it would have been rough for us. Leading Parker was always your destiny, and I would have been a distraction. Dead weight. And as much as I don't really want to say it, I think we're better off having not put ourselves through that. Struggle isn't love. I genuinely loved you. I'm walking back a better person."

"Walking back," I repeated. "Like... walking back to me? To our relationship? Like those seven years apart where I didn't even get to be your friend never happened? Is that what you want?"

The way he dipped his head and his gaze dropped to the floor, I felt bad. I didn't need to keep bringing it up, but I felt strongly that I would have been there for him if he would have let me. The decision to leave was his and his alone. The demons that he decided he needed to fight, he fought alone by choice.

I tapped his arm, then slid a hand until I gripped his bicep. I couldn't keep treating sensitive, feeling Malik like cold and steely Tony. This man wore his emotions on his sleeve and damned if I was going to bring more hurt to him, not when he'd come all the way here to make things right between us.

"I'm sorry. I know I sound like I'm still angry, but I'm not. At least, I don't want to be."

"I'll take it though. If you need to vent."

"Ancient history, Promise."

I gulped down a swallow of wine, then set the glass on a coffee table in front of us. I turned toward him, tucking my feet up under me and scooting closer. "Catch me up on what's new with Malik Hines, since you like to hide from headlines."

"Uh, okay. Well, for one, I wrote that game I was always talking about."

"The Black brothers in space?"

"Yep." He beamed, nodding with pride. "It's called Galaxy Bros: Mercury. It's a mobile game you can download on your phone."

"Like... in the app store? I can download it and play? Like right now?"

"Yeah. It's available. We premiere at this big indie game expo next month. I'm hoping to get Hines Tech in front of some influential people."

"*Indie* game expo?" I asked. I was interested in gaming to a very shallow point, which started and ended with Malik. Once we stopped dating, I stopped caring about the world of game development. "Wouldn't you want to sell it to like... X Box or something? There would be money in that, right?"

"Nah," he said, already shaking his head. "I mean, yeah, I could make some money selling flashy games to some big conglomerate. My game is mine, though. It means too much to me. I don't want anybody's hands in it— next thing I know, the characters will be frogs or some shit. You see how Hollywood does us in movies? Can you imagine how they'd treat a game with Black characters?"

"Ah..." I nodded, thinking about how Princess Tiana was a frog through most of Disney's The Princess and the Frog. "So, how would you sell the game?"

"I want to launch on a platform that's indie friendly. There's a few of them out there, but the money is funny. A certain cost to host the game, plus they take a cut of revenue." He wagged his head. "The deal has to be right, because that's just the beginning of what Hines Tech has to offer."

"I always knew this is where you'd be. And is there... any*one* keeping you out of trouble? Besides Brandon?"

He stared at me... then burst into loud laughter. "You're a straightforward person, India. You can cut this hinting shit. You want to know if I'm dating? Married? Otherwise committed?"

"I want to know if I'm pathetic," I said, reaching for my wine. I poured another swallow down my throat and continued. "I walked in on the man I've been dating— sort of— for three years fucking another woman today. If you came to my place to brag about how you found bliss with someone else, it would just be icing on the cake."

"Whoa, wait..." he said, holding out a hand to halt conversation. His eyes were wide and his top lip curiously curled. "You walked in on *Tony Clark* with someone else? Today?"

Slowly, I returned my glass to the table. "You really have been keeping track. Why do you ask?"

"It's...it doesn't matter. I'm sorry to hear about him stepping out on you. I gotta say what I always say when you get a new man...."

"That dude whack," I recited, dryly and with a roll of my eyes. "And you would not be wrong. Steena was sure that you were only coming over to brag about your beautiful wife and your perfect children and white picket fence and idyllic life.”

He chuckled. “I don't get a dog in your fake Stepford scenario?”

“Sure. Like a sheepadoodle. So you didn't come over here to brag about your happy suburban life?”

“I live in a warehouse loft and I'm pretty sure the fence out back is chain link. No wife, no kids, no... *doodle.* I have four twenty-somethings that I have to yell at to turn off the coffeepot, so they don't burn the warehouse down. It's a very much disjointed tech life.”

“You're really gonna make me ask, aren't you?”

He shook his head. “Ask...what?”

I reached out, then landed a hand on his thigh. And squeezed. His muscle flexed under my palm, then relaxed. “Why are you here, Malik?”

“Well...” he replied, his tone dropping so low I felt it rumble across my skin. “I was summoned. *In person. Very soon.*”

I grinned, blushing at the desperate tone he added when he recited my email back to me.

“I definitely didn't type it like you're saying it. We could have met for lunch tomorrow or had a Zoom date or—”

“Let's not pretend that I don't know you. You made it clear you wanted to see me tonight. And don't get it twisted, I didn't even think about declining. But I wouldn't be here if I wasn't invited. So I should ask you...”

He paused, drawing out the moment, playing with electric live wire between us. “Why am I here?”

“Because...because I haven't stopped thinking about you since I got those flowers,” I confessed. “My heart, my mind, my soul have wanted you to walk back into my life for a long time now.”

"Even though you had a thing going on with Tony."

"I went to see him to make *sure* the flowers weren't from him. And then I broke up with him. Because I wanted them to be from you."

"There's a part of me," he said, "that wants to argue that we are mature adults, that we can't go back, that we can't repeat history, that the years have changed us as people."

"Oh, that bitch is loud in the back of my mind. I can't be out here looking stupid, thinking we can pick up where we left off. But I also can't ignore the draw that's still between us. I know you feel it, too. I see it in your eyes."

His gaze flicked to my mouth, full and soft and stained from wine, then fell lower to my chest and the hardening nipples making themselves obvious. Slowly, his eyes rolled back up to mine and he licked his lips, confirming a simmering need without saying a word.

I leaned in, closing the sliver of space between us to cup his chin and draw his mouth close to mine, then pressed my lips to his. I held his face in my palms as his tongue urgently swirled and worked to possess mine.

I knew I wasn't the only one heating up. I saw it in the way his breathing quickened and the pulse at the base of his throat pulsed double time, the way his Adam's apple bobbed when he swallowed. There was nothing lost between us. The years we'd been apart dissipated, fizzled into a lusty fog.

"Just being honest here, because we both know what this is. You're here because I missed you and I hoped you missed me. The memories of what we had — the really good parts? The parts I've never forgotten? They've been swirling in my mind all day. All night. I have really missed fucking you. I have missed you fucking me."

I pulled back, but never dropped eye contact. Those hazel eyes bored into mine, full of hope and longing.

"I won't be upset at all if you get up, put your shoes on, and walk out. But there's a reason I invited you over. And there's a reason you didn't decline the invite. So... I'm going to my bedroom to get comfortable. I hope you follow."

CHAPTER EIGHT

THE WAY SHE ASKED *WHY ARE YOU HERE* TOLD ME EVERYTHING I needed to know.

She knew exactly why I'd sent the flowers. She knew why I had to email her to reveal myself. It was the only way that door was going to open. And why, when it did, I got in my car at 10 PM to see her.

I have missed fucking you. I have missed you fucking me.

After telling me she was going to get up and move to her bedroom, she unfolded herself and got up from the couch. Without a word, she walked away, past the glittering Christmas tree in the corner of the living room. Just before she rounded the bend into the next room, she glanced over her shoulder to make sure I was getting up.

I was. I followed, watching her hips send me into a trance with their sway.

She turned away from me as she entered the bedroom, a room awash in airy fabrics and muted colors with dashes of bold reds, purples, and blues for an accent. It was very, *very* India.

She pulled the gray cotton nightshirt over her head. I

couldn't wait to touch her. I had been craving the sensation of her skin on my fingertips and now she was so close I could reach out and run my hands across her shoulders. I shook with anticipation as I moved into place behind her.

When my fingertips brushed her shoulders, they sagged in relaxation. I trailed down familiar curves and caught the waistband of her leggings.

"You can get rid of those," she quietly suggested. So I did, hooking my thumbs in the elastic, and slid my hands down the sides of her body, taking the thin fabric with them. She stepped out of them and left them where they landed.

My eyes could not leave the landscape of her brown skin. I drank and drank and *drank it in* and I still couldn't get enough. She had gained some thickness in her waist, her hips, her thighs. I couldn't wait to feel them draped over my shoulders. Her shape was all I'd been dreaming about, and now my daydreams had become real life.

The India that had lived in my mind for seven years was replaced with this new, grown and sexy, fully adult version.

"I've really missed this," she whispered, tipping her head back to rest on my shoulder. "The pads of your thumbs always had callouses from the game controller. Your hands feel different from anyone else."

I closed my arms around her, pulling her closer to me, pressing my warm, growing length into her. The feeling, the attraction, missing these moments between us? It was mutual.

My hands roamed up to her breasts. They were plump, perfect orbs, the hard nubs of her nipples already standing on end. My mouth watered at the thought of brushing my tongue across the sensitive buds and hearing her pleasure in response.

I played, eliciting a light moan. Rubbing, teasing, playing, pinching, everything brought breathy gasps that made me harder. I stepped back, just long enough to pull off my hoodie and t-shirt. The sounds that rolled from her when she felt us reconnect... it was all I could do to not bend her over, grip her hips and push myself into her right there.

But I wanted to take my time. I had waited years for this moment, for this time with her. I could wait a few minutes more.

My hands moved faster, her heavy breasts bouncing as I held them in my palms and flicked my fingertips across her nipples. India's back arched, curving her body into mine I pushed my hips forward, giving her something to grind on.

She began a slow, circular wind. I caught her rhythm, grinding back until we were thrusting against each other. I slid a hand down her body to the warm, juicy valley between her thighs and pressed my middle finger hard against her clit before I used her wetness to tease her. Up and down, around and around and back again.

"Oh, God yes," she moaned, at the edge of a titillated, shaky sigh, and pressed herself back into me. Harder. Faster.

I chuckled into her ear. "If you think I waited seven years to dry hump and finger you, you've got a surprise coming."

I felt her cheeks round with her smile. "Then you should probably make your move, because I'm about to come."

I spun her around and dropped my lips to hers. Her mouth opened on instinct and our tongues danced together while my hands roamed the thick roundness of her ass and thighs, up her back and down again.

I pulled her deeper into the kiss, eking out every second

of pleasure until she finally pulled back, gasping for air. It gave me a chance to explore, so I tilted my head to plant kisses and light nibbles down her neck, across her shoulders while inching us toward the bed.

We hit the edge and toppled onto it, then rolled until she was on top, staring me down. Panting so hard, her breasts rolled with each breath. They were so tempting, and I couldn't resist a second longer. My mouth closed over one nipple and then the other, licking until she pebbled against my tongue. I worked the other with my thumb as I sucked like a hungry man.

I remembered she loved that. She loved to be sucked. *Hard*. Everywhere.

India writhed, grinding against the bulge in my sweatpants, her hard breaths almost drowning out her words. "You're the only one... that does it... right..."

I gave her nipples a reprieve to tug my sweatpants down. Before I could do the same with my briefs, India pulled them down until I sprang out at full attention. Her eyes lit up. I smirked, then almost came when I felt the wet warmth of her mouth.

She sucked slowly; I felt the vibration of her moans roll through me. Her tongue licked and swirled around the sensitive tip, then she took me in long, languid strokes.

My back arched—it was honestly the first good head I'd had in a long while and I wasn't sure how long I could hold out. My movement offered more of me to her wanting mouth, so she seized the opportunity, almost swallowing me, then pulling back.

"You still don't have a gag reflex, huh?" I joked through pants of pleasure.

"My ex said I gave weak head," she said, before taking me again.

"Are you serious?" I tipped my head up in time to watch her sink down on me, her thick lips wrapped around me. I loved the view. "Was *he* serious? Are you trying to prove him wrong right now?"

She laughed but didn't miss a stroke, bobbing faster and faster and *faster*. I watched the pure ecstasy cross her face— her eyes closed, both hands moving and working for my enjoyment.

And hers. She was enjoying the fuck out of herself.

"India," I warned, with a stuttered breath. "I need to come inside you."

She released me, then laid out next to me on her back. I sat up, grabbing up the pile of soft cotton I'd kicked off, found my wallet, then the condoms I had stuffed in there.

Just in case. Because how could I meet up with a woman I was sure I was still in love with and not take an opportunity to enjoy her body if it came up?

I unwrapped a condom, rolling it on while watching India in the middle of the bed with her legs wide, her hands palming her breasts.

"Hurry," she urged, her hands moving past her belly to her core. It was an incredible sight— India naked, one hand on her clit, the other working a nipple, a lusty half-glazed look in her eye.

I couldn't help myself. I dove between her thighs and closed my mouth around her clit.

She yelped in surprise... then opened her legs to give me room. I flicked my tongue up and down, around, across as light as a hummingbird. Both hands gripped my head; her body shook as the tremors took her higher each time my tongue made contact.

"Harder! Oh shit, suck me harder!"

I applied pressure, sucking like I was drinking the best

milkshake I'd ever had. Like my life depended on it. I moved from her clit to her pussy and back, driving her closer to the cliff, pushing her to the edge.

When I knew she was seconds from orgasm, I pulled back, moving up her body until I could rub the sheathed head against the wetness of her pussy.

She gave a whimper with each gentle push, then pull back.

"Malik...*please!* Don't tease me... I want it—"

Before she could finish her sentence, I pushed into her. I fought hard for control, but she was so warm and so wet and her pussy was already spasming around me. I couldn't help myself. Egged on by lustful, throaty yelps and the gyration of her hips to pull me deeper inside her, I hit a rhythm and held it, working like an oiled piston.

Her mouth fell open. Her eyes rolled back, then closed. She lifted her legs to open herself up wider. I hooked my elbows behind her knees and drove deeper. India grabbed my face and brought my lips to hers.

Harder!" she hissed, greedily, hungrily demanding. "This! This! I need this! Fuck me hard and make me come!"

Bolts shot down my spine. My temperature rose and beads of sweat joined the goosebumps that pocked my skin. I leaned in to kiss her and I felt... moisture.

I pulled back, surprised to see a tear roll down one cheek, then the other. Her eyes were closed, and her skin turned a red pallor.

"India! What's—"

"Don't stop! It's so fucking good and I haven't felt this fucking good in so fucking long. Please don't sto—"

A violent shudder rocked her; I doubled my efforts. She yelped, tightening her limbs around me, holding me close. I felt the tremble building from deep within her core. I wanted to bring her to the edge and fall over it with her.

She worked her hips and rode me from beneath. "Come with me!" She whispered, begging. "Come with me!"

"You go, I go," I answered. "Tell me when."

"Now!" she screamed. "Now, now, now...oh my God, yes!"

My thrusts became hard jabs to get as deep as possible. I erupted with her, burying myself inside her, unleashing everything I had to give.

India tossed her head back and let her climax overtake her, wave after wave rocking her body. I felt her pussy contract in massive earthquakes, milking me. I pushed in deeper still, just to be closer to her. She moaned louder, devolving into unintelligible mumbles.

I pushed up, but she closed her arms and legs around me again. "Not yet. I want to still feel you. Please, just stay here."

I relaxed, letting myself enjoy her skin. The firm smoothness of her, the warmth of her body, the way I felt wrapped up in her.

Bruh. If you gotta let this go again, you're gonna be in some serious trouble.

"You're so warm," she mumbled, her eyelids at half-mast. She tipped her head up and softly swiped her mouth across mine. I welcomed and deepened the kiss. The groan that rolled from her was enough to make me hard again.

"Careful. We'll be on our way to round two before you know it."

"I'm not saying that's a bad idea," she replied, stretching her limbs, and arching her back. "Was it always that good?"

"Not at first. I put a little spin on things— some special shit I've been cooking up."

"Malik," India whispered. "This isn't a one-night thing, right? You're not going to leave and disappear, and I never see you again?"

"You tell me," I answered. "*In person. Very soon.* You extended the invite."

"I don't want you to leave."

"Then I won't." I dropped a kiss onto her swollen, chapped lips. "This time, I'm not leaving unless you want me to."

CHAPTER NINE

india

The alarm that I forgot to turn off blared bright and early, 6 AM.

I reached for the phone to shut it off, but my palm landed on a warm chest instead. The blackout shades in my bedroom masked morning sunlight, necessary because my bedroom was on the east side of the building.

The lump next to me grumbled, then stretched, raising his arms above his head. I sat up quickly, afraid that the whole evening had been a dream and that I was in bed with Tony, except he rarely stayed over much anymore.

In a half-second, I realized I was not having a nightmare. The body next to mine was Malik. I laid a palm over my chest and willed my heartbeat to slow to a steady thump.

My inner thighs were deliciously sore, so last night *had* happened.

I crawled over him to the edge of the bed and turned off the alarm, then flipped the lamp on the lowest setting. My eyes landed on clothing scattered across the carpet, the condom wrappers littering the nightstand and a lukewarm, open bottle of water. We had mustered up just enough energy to grab a quick shower and roll into bed.

A heavy hand landed on my backside and squeezed the flesh, then smoothed down my thigh and between my legs. I grabbed the last condom, then maneuvered back to the middle of the bed.

I pulled the down comforter away, exposing us to the cool early morning air.

"You are still so fucking sexy in the morning." I hovered above him, noting his low cut fade, his disheveled beard, the curl of his lashes. The plump fullness of his lips. "Probably because you don't really sleep. You nap. What time do you usually get up?"

"Early. I can't stand to lay in bed if I'm not going to sleep. Or fuck."

"Oh, okay. Well, we're not sleeping, so…"

I settled astride his body and leaned in, dropping a whisper of a kiss on his forehead, then moving to his mouth. I felt his palms cup and gently knead my breasts, then his thumbs found my nipples and worked them until they were stiff nubs.

I had to stop nibbling his lips to giggle at the sensation. "Watch it. The nipple to pussy pipeline is always open. Don't start stuff you don't plan to finish."

He laughed. "Ima finish. This still makes you wet, huh?"

"Like turning on a faucet. You gonna do anything about it?"

"I don't remember you being this chipper at 6 AM," Malik mused, while his hands toured my thighs, soothing strokes up and down before slipping two fingers between my legs and burying them deep inside me.

My hips hunched involuntarily as he gently plunged and pulled back, then plunged again. His thumb pressed against my clit, sending shock waves throughout my core.

"Are you in a hurry?"

"Not… at all." I rode his fingers, galloping toward an early orgasm. "I don't have… to be… in early."

"So you got time, you're saying."

He groped for a breast and put my nipple in his mouth. My head rocked back. I let out a grunt of "*Shitshitshit, oh my God, right there,*" into the air.

He flicked the nipple, rasping the bud with his tongue, then asked. "You bout to come?"

"Yes, yes, yes, yes! Don't stop."

But he did. He withdrew his fingers and sat up, wrapped both arms around me and tipped us over. I whimpered. He soothed… then moved to settle between my legs. I felt him, warm and hard between us.

"I told you last night what I came here to do."

I produced the still wrapped condom. "Then you'll need this."

He snatched it, ripping it open, then sitting up long enough to roll it on. When his warmth and weight returned and he pushed into me, buried to the hilt, I was ready—legs already splayed, my pussy already thumping in anticipation.

I was a trembling, convulsing mess in a few hard, forceful strokes.

"Hey, Lover," he whispered, when I had come down long enough to hear him.

I was deliriously happy to hear those words in my ear. He bent to give me the softest, most romantic kiss.

Then braced himself on his elbows to crash his body into mine until he roared through a shuddering climax.

"I wish I would have thought to put your clothes in the wash last night. They could have been drying all morning. Now you have to go home in... that."

I gestured at his dirty sweats.

"Don't worry about it. I don't mind riding home with the essence of India on me." Malik paused in the hallway, his boxer briefs balled up in his fist. He was adamant that he was not putting dirty briefs back on. "Ima just have to free ball it and hope I don't get pulled over."

He leaned in to press his lips to mine in a sweet kiss. His free hand caressed me through my robe, then pulled me close enough to feel his length growing thicker, harder under his sweats.

"I have a conference call in a half hour, or I'd take care of that."

A light moan rose from his throat. "I wish you could, too, but I gotta go. Busy day at Hines Tech. I hope we'll talk later."

"Give me your phone."

I waited for him to fish it out of his pocket, unlock it, and hand it to me. I added my personal email address and mobile number and saved the entry. Then I called myself from his phone, grinning as I waited for my voicemail to pick up.

I handed him the phone. "Leave me a message to listen to later."

He frowned and cocked an eye at me. Then did as I asked and left a message on my voicemail. "Uh. This is Malik. You are...brilliant," he said, smiling. "Beautiful. Sexy as fuck. Thank you for opening the door. Thank you for not cussing my ass out. Thank you for the best night I've had in… about seven years. Save this number. I'll be calling you."

He hung up and pocketed the phone.

"You got no more times to delete me from your phone, Malik Hines. I *will* cuss your ass out if we have to have this chat again."

"I'm scared o' you."

"Should be. Yesterday I threatened to fire my entire staff. Ask about me."

"I don't have to. I know all about you, India."

I rose onto my toes to press my mouth to his again. Having him back in my life, my arms, my body, my bed had already spoiled me. I already didn't want him to go.

He leaned down to pick up his shoes and noticed the box sitting next to the door. "Is that going out to the dumpster? I can take it down for you."

"Oh. That's Tony's stuff. He's supposed to come and get it, but I doubt I'll see—"

A loud series of knocks sounded at the door. "India!" I heard from the hallway.

"You've got to be kidding me." I muttered, reaching for the knob.

"Hold up," said Malik, a hand on my arm. "Who is yelling in the hallway for you before 8 AM?"

"Tony," I answered. "Open the door. He's probably here for his stuff."

Malik positioned himself in front of me, then turned the knob and pulled the door open. For a moment, neither man said anything. Tony tried hard to look foreboding, but with his thin wire-framed glasses and receding hairline, he didn't hold a candle to Malik's sturdy physique, close-cut beard and full head of hair.

"Can I help you?" Malik finally asked.

"No. This is my girlfriend's condo. Where is India?"

"I'm right here," I called out, poking my head around Malik. "What's up, Tony?"

"What's up? We can start with why is this... *thug* is at your home at—" He stopped to pull back the sleeves of his designer tracksuit that he definitely never sweat in. "7:16 AM."

I felt Malik tense up. I laid a hand on his back, hoping to calm him. He had never been the fighting type, but I had never actually had two men facing off in front of me.

"Don't get slick at the mouth Tony," said Malik. "I haven't cut your check yet."

"What?" I poked my head around Malik again, thoroughly confused. "Catch me up. What check?"

"Malik is one of my patent clients," said Tony, his eyes never leaving Malik's face. "He owes me nearly ten grand."

"I've got five days left on your Net 10 invoice. You'll be paid; don't worry about it."

"Malik?" I glanced up at him, hoping my expression didn't accuse him of anything. "Tony is your attorney? Why would you do business with him if you knew we were dating?"

"I can trust anyone you trust," he answered. "I needed an attorney and when you started popping up with him, it put him on my radar. He got the job done."

"Who said I trusted him? He doesn't do any legal work for Parker."

"The question is," Tony cut in, "why you're here, at my girlfriend's place, early in the morning?"

"*Ex*-girlfriend," I corrected. "Malik and I knew each other in college. We go way back."

He eyed Malik in his clothes from last night, his bare feet, not to mention the briefs balled up in his fist and obvious semi-erection that told the entire story of what was happening.

I sensed his anger roiling, saw it in the flare of his nostrils and the curl of his lip.

"You want me to believe this is the first time you've seen him since college, and he just came out of your place looking…" He huffed, pushed his glasses further up the bridge of his nose and barreled forward. "You came to my office, presumably about some flowers, then picked a fight so we would break up."

"Picked a fight?" I laughed. "You were balls deep in some other woman when I walked in."

"Oh, please. You just happen to be entertaining your old college boyfriend this morning? You two have been fucking around, using me in some sick game—"

"Don't flatter yourself, Tony. If you're here for your things, they're in that box. Malik, would you hand it to him, please?"

"This box I thought was trash? Sure." He bent to pick up the box and pushed it into Tony's chest. Tony grabbed it before it could fall.

"India, we need to talk," He said, leaning to see me around Malik. "Alone. I've been texting you since last night—"

"No, thank you. We said everything we needed to say yesterday. You're making family moves, you're tired of my dad's lectures, our arrangement was childish and immature, et cetera and so on. I agreed, and we split up. The end."

"Maybe I was hasty. Maybe you and I can give a serious relationship a go. No fake girlfriend or boyfriend. No show for our families."

He stopped to level a glare at Malik. "Do you need to be here for this conversation?"

"Malik is my invited guest. He can be wherever he'd like to be. You and I are not having a conversation. You're taking your belongings and moving away from my front door. Good luck to you."

Malik snapped his fingers, pointing in Tony's direction. "Remind me... he was the dude that said you give weak head?"

"Mmhmm." I replied, giving a comedically large emphatic nod. "He also said it takes me forever to come when we fuck."

Malik laughed. "So, last night when you—"

"Sucked the soul out of you?"

"And then this morning when you—"

"Came in about six strokes?"

We glanced at each other, then both looked at Tony, then burst into laughter. He didn't seem to find the humor, but Malik and I had a gut level cackle as we watched him exhale a frustrated breath and take off down the hall with a cardboard box under his arm.

"Well." Malik glanced at me, a shy smile playing at the corners of his mouth. He looked up the hall one way and then the other. "Now your neighbors know you got dicked down last night."

"Oh. I think they had a clue before now," I added. "I hope they're happy for me."

He worked his foot into one shoe, then the other. "I hate to go, but Brandon has a code review this morning and I want to see how much progress we made last night."

"Let's not make that bossy, high yellow boy mad."

"You think I can see you later?"

"Highly possible." I cupped his chin and brought his

lips to mine for one last kiss. "Last night was the stuff dreams are made of. For real. I'm not ready to wake up."

"Me neither. We'll definitely talk later."

"Good morning, Evelyn! Wait, is it still morning?"

I sailed into the executive suite with a wide smile. It was a bright, beautiful, sunny December morning and Malik had ensured that I was in a very good mood when I left for work. It was unlike me to be late coming in, but my calendar was clear. And just because I wasn't at the office didn't mean I hadn't done any work. I spent over an hour on calls, answering email and querying the staff regarding the daily reports that hit my desk each morning.

"It's not yet noon, so good morning." She glanced at me over the rims of her square frame glasses that hung on a chain around her neck, her face lit by the glow of the tablet in the center of her desk. "Ms. Winters is waiting in your office. She's been in there for quite a while."

I opened the door to find Steena perched at the meeting table in the corner of the room, basking in the ray of sunlight that beamed through the window. I could see why my father loved this office. It was bathed in morning light, which was his favorite time of day.

"Well, good morning, sunshine," she said, directing a wide smile at me. "You don't even need to say anything. The blown back is all over your face."

"Hush," I hissed, pushing my door closed. "Evelyn doesn't need to know anything I don't tell her."

"Sorry. I was excited. I picked up some coffee for you."

She closed the lid of her laptop and pointed to a tall cup from Brew Bar, a shop that served coffee and coffee-flavored confections. It wasn't far from Parker, and we often walked down there when we needed a break.

I unpacked my bag and joined her at the table, sipping a bit off the top. "Ooh, that's good. Is this their new winter blend?"

"If you don't shut up about coffee and tell me what happened last night!" The glow in her eyes made me burst into laughter. "I can't believe you didn't text me until damn 9:30 and even then, didn't tell me shit but to meet you in here in an hour. And you're late."

"I'm not late," I joked, stalling by sipping more coffee. "I just wasn't here at dawn."

"Whatever. I've been in here for hours. Evelyn tried to kick me out twice! Tell me and leave in the juicy details. I know he came over there. He'd be a fool not to. How was it?"

"He made it around 11. Brought me wine, unlike my best friend."

"Bitch, I offered!"

"Yeah, well, he is a man of action. He didn't ask, he just did it. He's my same super smart, sexy geek, with more a of a salt and pepper look."

"Mmmmm..." She hummed. "I can see it."

"It's hot. He is still fine as hell. A little more built than he used to be. He's put on some weight." I shrugged. "So have I."

Steena rolled her eyes. "Boohoo. Your curves have curves, and you know you look good. So... *everything* went well?"

"Everything was..." I felt my eyes roll back in my head.

"We are definitely still a match. A lit match. A raging inferno."

"After seven years? Damn. I looked him up, you know."

That popped me back to reality. "Where? How?"

"Where and how do you think? You wasn't going to, so I did. We have to stay vigilant."

"Well, alright Inspector Gadget. And?"

She frowned. "Nothing! He's boring. No marriage certificates, no divorce certificates, no bankruptcies. He filed paperwork with the state for Hines Tech LLC. Private Instagram, no Facebook presence to speak of. Hines Tech is on twitter but it's a business account. Game updates. If he's on twitter personally, he's not loud about it. He's quiet."

"Good. I'm not worried about the Chronicle, but I also don't want them on my ass. Or up his."

"I guess he checks out then, if you like boring." She leaned in, brows hiked to her hairline. "Tell me about last night. Go slow."

"Nothing more to say than from the windows to the walls. I mean, not really. More like from the couch to the bed. But we had a very good time last night." I sipped my coffee with a smile, then added, "And this morning."

"Mmmhmm," she hummed again, adding sharp snaps of her fingers. "I haven't seen you this feisty in a while, Ms. Parker. Your ex-boyfriend needs to come around more often."

"Speaking of exes, guess who showed up as Malik was kissing me goodbye?"

"No." She frowned. "Because my only guess can be Anthonius Lavelle and I am tired of that man."

"Talking about he was trying to text me since last night because he'd been thinking that maybe we should make a real go of a relationship."

"A day late and several dollars short. That man needs to use his Black Platinum Rich Nigga Shit Credit Card to purchase several clues."

"He was so pissed to see Malik come out of my place this morning, both of us looking well-fucked in post coitus afterglow. And knowing full well he has never put this kind of smile on my face. I wish I got it on camera."

"So I sat in here for over an hour and all I get is confirmation that y'all did the do, the night actually ended this morning, and you already made your ex jealous?"

"I told you everything! What other details do you need, Steena?"

"Stop acting brand new; you know how we do."

"I know way too much about the men you date. I'm not hiding anything from you but you're not getting a play-by-play while my father's executive admin sits on the other side of that wall."

"Alright, fine. I'll respect your privacy at this time. But I expect more salacious details at drinks tomorrow."

"I thought you had an option."

She lifted and lowered a shoulder. "He fell through."

"I don't know how to feel about being your Plan B."

"You know you're always my Plan A, girl."

"I did actually have a business reason to meet with you, though. Something Malik said last night won't leave me alone and now I have ideas. I want to bounce it off of someone who won't reject everything I say because I was the one to come up with it."

"Aight." She leaned back, coffee cup in hand. "Shoot."

"So, Malik owns a game studio with one game out in the market already. He's looking at his options to produce more games in the series and future Hines Tech developments. And I started thinking..."

"Uh uh. India. No," Steena interrupted. "I'm going to stop you right there because no. You're not thinking about putting Parker money, or God forbid *your* money into your ex-boyfriend's little game. The dick was not that good."

"That's not what I'm talking about, first. And second, it's not a *little game*. If you have a phone, you can play it. That's... not little. After Malik left, I downloaded it, and I can't stop playing it."

I pulled out my phone and scrolled to the app to show her. The cartoonish characters and bright Galaxy Bros logo splashed across the screen. The music bed underneath was a shoulder bumping, rhythmic thump.

"It's cute, it's fun, it's challenging, but not hard. His team did a great job pulling you through the game— and the characters are Black! The next version of the game will be bigger and better and harder. Galaxy Bros could be a huge deal and I'm just thinking about how to be a part of that. Remember yesterday when I said I wanted something new to work on? I'm craving an exciting project, something our younger demographic will grab onto. We need to do something we haven't done before that could push us into new territory."

"I see your point. But is Malik asking you to invest?"

"No. But he's an indie game developer. He wants a way to distribute that lets him retain ownership. At the same time, Parker's reach taps out at Millennials and most of us are turning forty. What if we could be a source for independent gamers? If the games are built for streaming, all they need is a code to access a game that lives... somewhere. Preferably a server that Parker owns. If they're console games, we can sell the actual games at the kiosks."

"I remember my brothers getting games at like...

Walmart. And Game Stop. What's to stop people from just buying them there?"

"Nothing, if they're for sale there. Game Stop is a point of sale. They don't *publish* games. That's not where those games live, especially if they're not tied to a console. And they're not Parker. And they're not Black owned."

"Hmmm. See, I don't know anything about this to know if it's a good idea or not. Is there a market?"

"That's just it, Steen. We create the market. What's to stop us from using a subscription-based model and improving on it to focus on independent Black game developers? That's a niche we can corner. I know we need answers but having questions is the exciting part. I'm thinking about writing something up for Business Development to see how fast we can move."

"You know Quinn is still pissed about how the Kiosks rolled out."

"I also know he's too close to retirement to leave. He needs to keep his job. So? Thoughts?"

"Well... I am inclined to think you have a good idea..." She paused, wincing.

"But?"

"Honey, I'm sorry, but you're sleeping with the man who would benefit. Nobody is going to look at this situation and think the best of you. I hope you don't think you need to do this to save him. Or to keep him. Who's to say he didn't reach out to you hoping for Parker to dump some money in his lap?"

"Steena—" I almost bit my tongue to keep myself from cursing her out in my office. "I'm not saying your points aren't valid," I continued slowly, barely managing my tone. "I'm saying I don't think they apply here. We talked about his need to secure hosting for his games. He didn't ask me for money or help—"

"He wouldn't! That's how it works. He would just casually drop a hint that he needs money, or he needs someone to generously offer to publish his games, if only he could find someone to do that for him. And then you do what you're about to do— swoop in and rescue him. Remember what I said about the Chronicle? You have eyes on you."

"Galaxy Bros premieres at some big expo in a few weeks. He's hoping to meet people who can give him some shine and back his studio so he can publish more games. Why can't that be Parker? Why can't we help each other?"

"Because that's love and not business. And just barely, because I promise you need to get to know this dude all over again."

She slid her laptop off the table and tucked it into the crook of her elbow, then stood.

"I want this second chance at love or rekindling or whatever y'all are calling it to work out for you. I really do. I hope he has good intentions and I'm the paranoid and overprotective friend. But I'm not a bullshitter. Remember why he left your ass the first time and learn the lesson."

At that, I felt my world screech to a halt. Did she really say that shit?

"Steena, I respect your opinion, but you're dancing on the edge of my nerves and my patience right now, not to mention your role with respect to who I am to you inside this building."

"I'm sorry, India. But you know I'm right." The edges of her mouth bent south, and slowly, she shook her head. "You're such a golden retriever about Malik. You always have been. You want to paint this like new business for Parker, and you *might* have a point, but I see right through you. Before you stick your neck out for this man that you've only been reacquainted with for a day, slow your roll, get some perspective, and make a *business* decision, not a heart decision. Otherwise, the executive staff is going to burn you alive, and not even being Bronson's daughter will save you."

Tʜᴇ ʙʟᴇssɪɴɢ ᴏғ ᴡᴏʀᴋɪɴɢ ᴡɪᴛʜ ʏᴏᴜɴɢ, ᴘᴀʀᴛ-ᴛɪᴍᴇ ᴡᴇʙ developers was that none of them were early morning people. I made it home in time to change, run a brush over my hair and comb through my beard, take care of my morning routine and fumble with the coffeepot before the team arrived.

I usually had the studio to myself for a few hours in the morning. Between 9 and 10 AM, people would filter in for the day. In the evening twilight, the headcount would drop until it was just me and, occasionally, Corey overnight.

I had shuffled to my office with my coffee and a tumbler of ice water and was deep into my daily habit of reading and filing away news stories to read later.

No pings on my India Parker google alert, I noticed. I wasn't sure how long I needed to keep that subscription active. I really only used it to keep up on how she was doing. Thanks to the previous day's bravery, I could get my news first-hand now.

"Yo, Malik."

Brandon thumped down the hall toward my office and

stood in the doorway in light blue work coveralls with Hines Foreign Auto emblazoned down the sleeves. He was stocky and broad-shouldered like Dad, but had inherited our mom's light, freckled skin tone and her wiry hair. He also had enormous feet, so the steel-toed boots he had to wear at the shop made the floor shake with each step. I heard him before I saw him.

"Yo, B." I spun around in my chair to face him. I tipped my head in a nod as he dropped into the chair in front of my desk. "You working a full shift today?"

"Yeah. We're finishing up an engine rebuild on a Porsche 911 and it'll go faster with two hands. I need to get it out of the shop today. Clarissa has some holiday reception for her job tonight, so I can't work late. She's getting the top performer award, so we have to go, I guess."

Brandon's fiancée Clarissa was the talented real estate agent that located and contracted the lease for the warehouse. I owed so much to her and couldn't wait until she was officially family, rings and all. The event was planned for next summer, but Brandon was getting antsy and hinting at eloping just so he didn't have to squeeze himself into a tux.

"You guess. Tell Riss I said congrats." He emitted a grunt in the affirmative and got up. "Hey, wait. So you won't be around tonight either? What's happening with the team, then?"

"That's why I came in early. I wanted to see how far Corey got on the fixes I gave him. He did a good job last night."

"Yeah, he was kicking ass, from what I could see. How far down the bug list did he make it?"

"He kicked it way down. I think the big errors that would stop a game are pretty much taken care of. I gave the team a list to go through level by level today since I'll be out. I'll check it out tomorrow."

"I can check it out, B. I know this shit, too."

"Yeah, but you know too much. You'll nitpick and get ideas and make more work. I told them to get the prototype ready for you to go through the game, front to back. Let's see what's still hanging out."

I pretended to be hurt, but I wasn't, and Brandon knew it. I designed his role to keep me away from the developers for the mental health and stress level of all involved. I was happy to stay above the fray, write and design the game, leaving the programming and detail work to the team and Brandon loved being in the thick of it.

"Fine," I finally answered, like the response was ever going to be different. Brandon got his way every time. "I'll hide in here, then if me being out there makes them nervous."

"You don't make them nervous. You derail progress with ideas that don't bring any benefit, and then we have to walk it back. That wastes time they could spend on other things."

"It's my name on the game. I just want it to be the best it can be!"

"My name is on it too. We all want that, but there's a method to the madness, so let them work the method. You feel me?"

"Yes. I feel you."

"Good. Glad we had this chat. So uh…" He sniffed, super casual. "Where'd you disappear to last night, playa?"

I'd been poking through the code in the sandbox, something Brandon hated. My head popped up at his question, though. I had hoped to keep my evening on the low, but I forgot men gossip more than women do.

"Huh?"

"You're not deaf, motherfucker. Where did you disappear to? Corey said you left around ten and you didn't come back before he dipped out at four. Where was you at all night?"

"Man," I said, sucking my teeth. "Corey can't keep nothin' to himself."

"Where'd you go?" Brandon pressed.

"I went to see a friend."

"A *friend*?"

"Yeah. A friend."

"All night. You went to see a friend and was out all night."

"I can't leave the studio?"

"Can? Yeah. Do you?" He laughed. "Rarely. You live at work and you're a homebody. Even if you go to the gym, you're back in... a couple hours. You ain't go to no gym all night. You don't prowl bars and shit. Ain't too many spots you can be *all night.* So where did you go?"

"Brandon... why are you asking?"

"Because I think this friend is named India Parker."

My jaw dropped. "How the hell—"

"Because you're my brother and I've known you my whole life, including the entire time you've known India Parker. I know that look," he said. Then added, "Your face says you saw her. All night."

"Get the fuck outta here, B. Who told you?"

"Man, Riss and I saw Pam and her husband last night. She asked if you called India so I had to get the whole scoop, 'cause I knew your ass was acting funny. You called her?"

"Nope, I didn't." Technically, I didn't. And I still hadn't, though I needed to.

"She called you?"

"Mmmmm... no."

Brandon's face broke out in the widest grin. "What the fuck? This is ridiculous. You don't want to talk about India?"

"Not in particular, no. I didn't even confirm it was India."

"But we both know it was."

I said nothing. What was there to say?

"So..."

"So... what? Get out my office, man."

"Nah, I need the update. As much as you have mooned over this woman for the last... however many years it's been since y'all split, I deserve the details. How's she doing? I know you stalk her."

"I don't stalk her. I sent flowers to her office. You know, the nice ones she likes. I emailed to follow up, made sure she got them and she knew they were from me."

"Uh huh. Made up a reason to talk to her. She replied?"

"She did. We had a little back and forth and she was like... hey you should come over." I shrugged, leaning back in the chair. I sensed Brandon delighting in my discomfort.

"And you do whatever India Parker wants you to do. You already so whipped, bro."

"She's a night owl. I was up I wanted to see her. I wasn't going to say no."

"Wouldn't recommend it. And?"

"And... I went over. Brought her some wine. We had a good talk."

"Fucked. Right? I hope you did."

"B—"

"Bro. Ain't no way you was in the same spot as India and y'all just talked all night. We both know what transpired, but you're playing shy. What time did you do the walk of shame out of her place?"

"Look, I'm an adult and you are not Dad. I'm allowed to not be home at night."

"Sure. sure."

He nodded, pulling his bottom lip between his teeth. I knew Brandon, though. He played too much.

"So like… it's not a hit and quit thing, is it?" He asked after a few moments. "Y'all back together or what?"

"What's with all the questions? We should be talking about Venus—"

"Don't change the subject. I'm trying to figure out if I can be happy for a nigga."

That made me laugh. "Yeah. Be happy for a nigga. We might have a good shot this time around."

"You had a good shot last time around. India wasn't goin' nowhere. That was all you. Don't fuck this up."

"Hey, listen though…" I sat up, kicking my feet to the floor. "Tell the team to take the night off. I'm thinking about inviting her over. I want to show her the studio, demo the game, let her see what I'm working on."

"Show off that big brain. End up in the loft. Should I tell the team to come late tomorrow, too?"

Brandon was saying whatever he thought would get a rise, and I was playing right into his hands. "Whatever, man," I replied, giving up the fight.

"Yo, I'm happy for you and Ima let you finish, but keep it light. We can't afford distractions. You can get hot and heavy after GameBox Expo. We need to be ready."

I glared across the desk. "I know you're not lecturing me about being ready for GameBox Expo."

"Ain't nobody lecturing. I'm just saying we have to be ready."

"Get out of my office and go to work. And protect your hands. I need them. I promise to stay in here and not bother your team." He pushed himself up from the low chair with a grunt. "I'm going through the game tonight, though, top to bottom. I'm taking notes. Make sure they know."

"I'm not going to tell you again to get out of the sandbox," he said, before thumping to the door. "I'm going to put kid safety locks on your login."

He left my office. And I logged out of the sandbox.

When Brandon left my office, I pulled my phone from the charger. Since India added herself to my contacts again, it was time to make good use of her number.

> Malik: Hey, Lover...

> Malik: is that old yet? :)

A few seconds rolled by before I saw dots bouncing to indicate that she was replying.

> India: Hey Lover...

> India: Old? No. :)

> India: It's been forever since I saw those words pop up on my phone. I missed them.

> India: I was just thinking about you. Actually, I haven't stopped thinking about you.

> Malik: I've been looking forward to typing them and actually pressing send.

Malik: Just saying hey.

Malik: And let you know I was thinking about you. And about last night. And about this morning. Do you still want to get together tonight?

India: Are we talking about getting *together*? If so… yes.

Malik: Is this your personal or corporate line? I need to know how nasty my response can get.

India: LOL! This is my personal line. Be as nasty as you wanna be. I look forward to returning the favor.

Malik: Aight, then. So remember how I used to make you play video games when you came over?

Malik: And that's why we had to study at your house?

India: That's not why we had to study at my house.

India: You never had any good food, and you bought your couch off Craigslist.

India: and you were easily distracted by video games.

Okay, yeah. Now I remembered. India was unimpressed by frugality.

India: but yes, I remember. Why?

Malik: Throwback. I want you to come to the studio. It's not EA Games in here or anything, but I'm proud of what I've built. I want to show it off. You can see the game in real time and preview the next evolution.

India: I'd love to see the studio! I downloaded Mercury and now I can't stop playing. This could be dangerous.

Malik: Ha, really? That's what's up. We can play the new game. And then I have some ideas on all the ways we can get *together*

India: :) All the ways? Care to be specific?

Malik: I promised B I'd leave the team alone, so I'm hiding in my office. I have time if you do.

India: I have a few minutes before my next meeting. My eyes, among other things... are wide open

Malik: So, I'm kind of always writing a game. I was thinking about last night like a choose your own adventure type thing.

India: LOL... I can't wait to hear this

Malik: So...like

Malik: remember when you took your top off. And I took off your leggings

India: mmmmhmmmmmmmm

Malik: what if...what if I had just bent you over right there

India: I would have liked it.

India: why didn't you?

Malik: Right place, wrong time. We had other adventures to get to.

Malik: But uh…

Should I say this??? She said I could be nasty. *Fuck it.* I thumbed out the message and hit send.

Malik: I'm hard as shit right now. Thinking about when I can fuck you from behind with your titties in my hands.

The dots bounced with fury, but when she replied, she only posted:

India: So what else are you thinking about?

I paused, listening for any... commotion outside my door. It was quiet in the office. I kicked back in the chair and got comfortable.

Malik: I'm thinking about you in your corner office, Ms. CEO.

Malik: Maybe I call you and tell you I want your leg propped up on the desk and your fingers in your pussy, and I walk you through everything I want you to do for me. And listen while you do it.

Malik: I'm thinking about how sexy it is for you to come for me, in your office, with all those folks that work for you walking around, not knowing what I'm doing to you.

After a few moments of no messages, a photo arrived in the chat.

India was in her office, one hand demurely hiding her smile. She was at her desk, her face lit by the afternoon sun, in dark jeans and a button up blouse over a silky white camisole. Imprinted in the fabric of the camisole were the unmistakable points of two erect nipples.

I groaned aloud. I loved knowing that the thought of even touching them sent her into a horny fugue.

Malik: Why you send me that? So I can think about how it feels to have them in my mouth?

India: You needed to know that you're sending me to a meeting with these damn diamond tips. What do you have to say for yourself?

Malik: You gave me permission.

Malik: You said I could be nasty. I was holding back, to be honest.

India: Don't hold back.

India: If I could, I would be in here with my jeans unzipped and two fingers buried deep while I read your texts to me.

Malik: that's so unprofessional, Ms. CEO

India: and that's why I haven't, lol! A girl can dream, though.

India: and I am dreaming.

Malik: Save it for later.

Malik: You wanna know what I just thought about?

India: Yes.

India: Tell me!

Malik: me on my knees with my face in your pussy and your thighs locked in the perfect position to make me suck on your clit until you're riding my face.

Dancing dots appeared. Then nothing. Then dancing dots. Then nothing.

Malik: too much?

No response.

Malik: India...

India: ...Malik?

Malik: ... yes?

She added a gif of one of those ladies from that show my grandma used to love, spritzing herself with a water bottle.

India: .... hard?

I laughed, thumbs working overtime.

Malik: Baby...

Malik: hard.

India: Shit. I gotta go.

Malik: LOL. Can't take it?

India: I can take anything you're offering for the record.

India: But my next meeting is starting in a few minutes, and I need to hit the ladies' room.

Malik: Have fun stuffing your bra so your nipples don't show.

India: No, I'm keeping those. But I have… pressing matters below the waist to take care of.

India: I want to hear the other adventures.

Malik: I'll text you an address and see you around 6. We're gamers tonight, so wear something comfortable.

Malik: And easy to take off.

I set the phone on the charger, then pushed my chair back to take in the view of my obvious arousal. It looked like I wouldn't be leaving my office for a while. I scooted back up to the desk and opened a browser window, navigated to my YouTube bookmark and then scrolled to a playlist of gaming company CEO interviews I'd been saving up.

"Nothing kills an erection like a lecture on code migration standards and firmware upgrades," I muttered to myself.

india

I AVOIDED STEENA MOST OF THE DAY, WHICH WAS WEIRD BECAUSE we had been joined at the hip for years. We were the closest of friends since junior high. Right after I took over operations for Parker, the company Steena worked at went left... and so did she. I brought her on to work with me and she had been a perfect fit for the organization. She even succeeded me as VP of operations.

We had never had a business disagreement until now. I could see her hesitation, but if it was about anyone but Malik, she would think Parker Games was the best idea I'd ever had. I was savvy enough to recognize the opportunity, but Steena refused to take her friendship blinders off to see the vision.

I spent a few hours after Malik left my place and all day between meetings looking at platforms, marketing, and what it took to become a publisher. Everything I read boosted my enthusiasm, and I resented the idea that I couldn't separate my brain from my heart. Steen was right. I had a keen eye for business. My concern was if Malik would partner with Parker.

> Malik: The studio is 999 West Indiana Ave.
> But park in the deck a block up.

> Malik: Your car will be safer there than on
> the street and I'll pay for your parking. The
> building is a gray brick two-story
> warehouse.

> Malik: can't miss the Hines Tech sign over
> the door. See you at 6.

I got his text with the address to the studio and my heart nearly leaped out of my chest. I hadn't looked forward to a Friday so much in a very long time. I sent Evelyn home early in a car and packed up my office to leave.

"Hey. India."

I looked up to see Steena in my doorway in her casual Friday jeans and blouse, a stylish computer bag over her shoulder. I went back to packing my bag.

"You made yourself clear this morning, Steena. It's not like I was going to hand over a wad of cash tomorrow. I will take your advice and do my research. Just save the lecture, alright?"

"I know. I'm sorry I even went there this morning. I know you will do the right thing because that's what India does. I came back up here to say I think I was just... emotional. It took you a long time to let Malik go, and I don't want you to get hurt. But I was out of line. Can I..."

I waved her in. She walked in, then sat in one of the guest chairs at my desk. I abandoned my bags and walked around to sit in the other one. I'd make time for an apology.

"You know I'm your strongest supporter, and you and I have always worked well together. I can't say that out of one side of my mouth, then criticize you and make crass commentary about your love life out the other side. I know good and well if Quinn had said that shit this morning, security would have had to walk me out."

"Thank you, Steen. I appreciate that you came back up here, because I was about to be petty about it tomorrow. And you know Quinn is scared of you. He wouldn't dare if you were in the room."

"He better not say that shit. So I shouldn't either. I'm sorry, boo."

I grabbed her hand and squeezed. "I know. And we knew a long time ago that the friend-employee line was going to blur. It was different when we were kind of on the same level, but we're in new territory now. I expect you to abide by the same standard I ask of the rest of the staff. I appreciate the acknowledgment that your words were out of line."

I tapped her hand and released it. "I also, unfortunately, think you're right."

I knew Steena was shocked to hear those words. So was I, to be real. My nerves wouldn't let me sit, so I stood up and paced in front of the floor to ceiling windows that lined my office.

"Even if it wasn't Malik, it would be *someone*. I need to treat this like taking on any partner. When it comes to developing this idea, what happens in my personal life, my time after hours can't have any bearing on my professional endeavors. We don't talk about him here, we don't joke about him here. I'll do my due diligence, and make the reveal when the time is right, but it won't be fair to Malik if I have to fight through bias to get a good idea on the table."

Steena agreed, her head bobbing in a nod. "You're right about the approach. And I hope all of it works out the way you want it to."

"Me too. It could work out well for us. It could help developers like Malik if we build it right."

"So, it looks like we had the same idea to leave early. Are you walking out?'"

"Yep, I'm out."

I finished packing, grabbed my bag and followed Steena out of my office, pulling the door shut behind me. It looked like most of the staff on the floor had left early as well.

"So you...have evening plans?" Steena asked, one brow hiked curiously as we arrived at the elevator.

I smiled to myself, thinking back to Malik's texts. Maybe he had a point about needing those years to work, to put his head down, to develop himself. The old Malik would have never said those things to me. I wasn't sure the old India would know how to receive them.

The Malik and India of today, seven years later, though? We were about to make up for so much lost time.

"Yeah. I do. I'm hoping to get some research in."

"Should be a good time."

The elevator opened on the basement level inside the underground parking garage. We had arranged our parking spots to be right next to each other, so we marched through the concrete structure toward her Range Rover. My sleek. BMW sat next to it.

She unlocked her vehicle and tossed her bag into the backseat, then used the remote to start it up. It roared to life, lights flashing, seats moving into place. "You'll be seeing the studio tonight, right?"

"Yes. He wants to show me the next game that's coming from Galaxy Bros. I want to get a feel for what it would take to be a publisher without having to drill him with questions. You know Malik will not want any part of Parker

Games at first. I don't want to tell him about my idea until I have it put together."

"Maybe you can convince him to be the guinea pig."

I cringed. "He won't like that. He's always been concerned about it looking like he's riding my coattails. But if it's not Malik, it'll be someone, so I'd just rather Hines Tech be the first publisher on the platform."

"Well, head on home, shave and moisturize and perfume everything." She grinned and backed away toward her car. "We both know what y'all are gonna end up doing. Call me later. Catch me up."

"Night, Steen. Love you."

"Love you back."

I ducked into my car and pressed the ignition button. Then smiled as I pulled out of the deck and pointed the car home.

I arrived at the address that Malik had texted me and followed his instructions to park in the deck. I walked the block to a nondescript gray brick building. The navy blue Hines Tech logo was painted onto a bright white sign that hung on the side of the building.

I pressed the button for the bell and a loud buzz rang out. A few moments later, one of the double doors opened and Malik stood just inside in a long-sleeved shirt with the Galaxy Bros logo across the chest, loose, dark blue sweats and socks on his feet.

I stepped inside, and into a warm, tight hug I didn't want to end. Malik smelled like rugged handsomeness, linen, and laundry detergent. He felt like coming home.

"Finally," he murmured, closing the door behind me, walking me backward so I was pinned between him and the door. I already felt him between us, as rigid as I'd left him that morning. "You made it."

"I did. Hi." I slipped my hand around the back of his neck and drew him close to me. Our mouths met in a slow, lingering, simmering kiss. His hands were already roaming, sliding around to my backside encased in my favorite pair of leggings. I wore a long t-shirt, minimal makeup and no jewelry.

I was so excited to be warm and comfortable, not dressed to the nines for some boring, perfunctory appearance with Tony, where we had to pretend we were a happy dating couple that didn't just snip at each other in the car.

When he pulled back from the kiss, he didn't go far. "I could get used to this again. Quickly."

"Me too. And I need you to come up off of one of these shirts for me." I tapped the logo that covered his chest.

Malik glanced down at his shirt. "You want my clothes already? This is one of the first designs we came up with. The newer ones are much nicer. I can probably dig one up for you."

"All I'm saying is that I need a Galaxy Bros t-shirt in my possession."

I pushed him back so I could kick off the Crocs I'd worn on the drive over and handed him the canvas bag I had unashamedly packed with toiletries and a change of clothes.

"Is anyone here?"

"Just us," he answered. "You want a tour?"

"Please. I already love this space."

Malik led me around the warehouse that had been renovated into a comfortable, laid-back studio. The ceilings were high with wood beams crossing the expanse of the space. Lighting fixtures hung every few feet, illuminating the different work and play areas. On one side, floor to ceiling whiteboard walls were covered with handwritten code, notes, reminders, and drawings. On the other side were smaller offices and workspaces.

In the center were open tables and cubicles. "This is where the magic happens," Malik said, pointing to the mass of monitors, cables, screens, keyboards. "Game-wise at least. The developers work here, play here. We have a Twitch station— that's where we have testers come in and play the game, stream it for their followers. That happens here too."

He led me further down the long, narrow space to a lounge area which looked markedly different from the rest of the warehouse. It was closer to a living room— plush carpet, deep set couches and overstuffed chairs, and two 80-inch screens mounted side by side over a cabinet that held every kind of gaming console I'd ever heard of. And some I hadn't.

"Wow." I bent to peruse the collection. "Is that a real Nintendo? Does it still work?"

"That's Brandon's. And yeah. He babies that thing. He doesn't really let anyone else play with it. We've got the usuals— X Box, PlayStation, Dreamcast. A couple of off-brand models too and some PCs so we can test out those games. We need to know how every console and platform works."

"So, will Venus work on all platforms?"

"That's the goal. And let me show you how." He walked over to the TV, pulled something from the side and brought it to me. It looked like my Fire stick. "So, I'm playing a game. You call me to come over. When India Parker calls, what happens?"

"Malik moves," I answered, grinning.

"Right. So I save my game, pull this stick— we're calling it the Play Anywhere Game Stick right now. I grab my controllers—"

He pointed at two small ergonomically shaped devices with buttons and knobs. "And roll out. I get to your house, and provided you have an HDMI port on your TV, plug it in. It rings up the game on the platform where it's hosted, connects to my universal controller via Bluetooth, and I resume my game. But now I'm at your house, up under your ass. Eating your food, drinking your beer..."

"Which is where I prefer you to be. But what happens if my TV doesn't have an HDMI port?"

"Then I pull it up on mobile. Or PC. Or drag my console with me, but the stick is designed to make the game portable. This device is what we just patented. Gamers have a lot of options and more than one way to play a game. To me, it doesn't make sense to make a game that isn't platform agnostic."

A platform agnostic game could also make it challenging to publish. But looking at that stick made my brain almost explode. I made a mental note to consider the retail options. It would make the perfect item to stock in the mall kiosks.

"Anyway," he said, plugging the device back into the TV. "This is where we hang out when we're just chilling, having fun, watching movies. Which... is never. The guys come in, work, leave. They don't want to hang around a dude that's almost 40."

"I want to hang around a dude that's almost 40."

He grabbed my hands and pulled me in, wrapping them

around his body, then closing his arms around me. I was tall enough to brush my lips against the dip in his neck.

"Even though he's one of those nerdy types that only talks about video games and writes computer programs for fun?"

"Mmmhmm..." I opened my mouth to nip at his skin with my teeth. "Did he already forget that he's the type that texts you the sexual adventure scenarios that he made up?"

I felt his laughter roll up from his belly. "I forgot I told you about those in my moment of horny vulnerability."

"I don't mind your horny vulnerability. It's very... very sexy."

"So, I have one more spot I need to show you that I hope you'll like."

He took my hands in his and led me back through the warehouse to the other end. "Kitchen's over there," he pointed, passing it. "It's functional, not worth a stop, but I did stock up today."

We headed to a set of stairs and climbed them to the second level. Once we reached the landing, he stopped and turned to face me.

"Every day, I get up and look over the warehouse from right here. From this vantage point, it's small, but there's so many good things coming from this space. And I'm really proud of it."

"You should be."

I joined him at the banister and smiled at the world Malik had created with mostly his own two hands. His pride was inspirational. And sexy as hell.

"I really am touched that you wanted to show me how you're living out your dream. Hines Tech is going to do big things. I can't wait to say that I watched it start right here."

"It didn't start here, though. It started back in college,

when I'd tell you about what I wanted to do with my life and you never pushed me to pursue another career path, to have a Plan B to get a *just in case* degree. When I say you played a part in this happening, I mean it, India."

"You're built for this and you're the one that built it. I just believed you could."

He leaned in to kiss me and I welcomed his lips, his touch, the gentle slide of his hand up and down my body, like he had already memorized my curves again. When the kiss ended, he slid a hand down my arm until our hands were clasped together.

"I saved the kind-of- best for last," he said, leading me through the open concept landing. "These are my living quarters. I don't spend a lot of time up here, but no one else on the team is allowed upstairs. Not even Brandon. This is like walking into my apartment."

"So you... live above your office."

"Essentially, yes. This building had been vacant for a few years, so we had to renovate. But I wanted it because it was already set up with a private room and the plumbing up here was already done. Being here keeps me close to the work and the team."

"I would never relax if I lived at Parker."

A light chuckle sounded from him as he gently pulled me toward a closed door. "Hence why I don't sleep. It's a double-edged sword but we wouldn't be where we are if we didn't get this building and I couldn't live on site. When I sleep, it's in here."

He opened the door to an open, airy space. Shades were drawn over the most of the windows, but a few were open enough to the view of a wooded area in twilight behind the building. High ceilings and wood plank floors covered by a dark gray rug were complemented by the charcoal gray accent wall behind the platform bed, which was neatly but simply made.

"It's very manly in here, Malik. Grey and black. Mature. Serious."

"You say that like you expected me to have a toy car bed and a Super Mario Brothers comforter set."

"In my defense, it looks like you stopped buying furniture on Craigslist," I teased.

"When we know better, we do better. This is where I hang out. Pretend to sleep. Think about you."

"I love it." I walked the length, poked my face through the blinds to check out the view, ran my hands long the furniture. "It's minimalist. It fits the space. And it fits you."

"You trying to say I'm simple?"

"You have the necessities and not a lot of clutter. You don't need frills. Extras."

"You haven't seen my office." He crossed the room to stand in front of me. Then stepped in closer, so close our bodies were touching. "Are you a frill or a necessity, India?"

I pretended to cringe. "You are not going to say that you need me right now, are you?"

"But I do. Did you know that yesterday I was literally just sending flowers to an old friend? The last... what? Twelve hours have turned my life upside down. And now I need to take advantage of every second I have with you, because I've missed so many."

"You aren't the only one that missed them."

We kissed, lightly at first, but as the kiss began to deepen, I stepped back and spun around. "What's the plan for tonight? Because if we don't get away from this bed, we won't be eating until midnight."

"If it was up to me, we'd spend the whole night up here

because I have seven years of not fucking you to make up for. And you did say you missed that."

"I did say that. And it *can* be up to you."

"I'll take you up on that later. We have other adventures we need to choose right now," he replied with a smile. "Let's go play."

"Do the Galaxy Bros have names?" Malik laughed. I gave him a side eye. "What? It's a valid question. The Super Mario brothers have names."

"I'm not laughing at you; you're just funny. The taller one is Roy. The shorter one is...Jay. Guess where we got the names."

I pondered for a minute, then shrugged. "Where?"

"What's my middle name? What's Brandon's?"

"Oh my God... Roydell and James! Genius."

"Yeah, we thought it was a nice way to pay homage to our parents."

"Wait. Did that character just say '*Bet*' when I selected the next level?"

I paused play on the game, freezing my characters mid-flight, and glanced over at Malik.

We were lounging on the couch in front of the big screen TVs. He did a quick run through of the game while we ate cheesy pasta and fresh, crusty bread from West End Pizza, Pasta and Subs, then he gave me a controller so I could play.

I was having a ball. It reminded me of hanging out with Malik in his dorm room, reading for whatever test I had to take while he played video games. After we were a couple, he would insist on at least one night a month where he taught me how to play one of his games. I never put much effort into it and usually gave up after a couple of levels. I preferred to watch him master the levels and discover the Easter eggs.

"Do you think it's too much? I've been going back and forth with Brandon on it. There's a thin line between cute and pandering."

"I don't think it's pandering," I said, unfreezing and moving along. "Stuff like that sets the game apart from everyone else. Besides, name a game that doesn't have some cheesy saying like *let's go* or *rock on*. It works."

"I trust your opinion. What do you think so far?"

"I think I'm wondering why this game isn't for sale yet. It's kind of hard, but not in a bad way. You think it's easy because it's so bright and fun, but damn, I'm struggling on this level. I like the music too."

"There's a couple of guys I contracted to license music just for this game. They did a lot of the sound effects, too. I want everything to be an authentic experience."

"You put a ton of work into this. What do *you* think of it??"

"Glitches aside, I like it. I think it turned out nice." The look he gave me made me want to cry— he was so proud. "I could nitpick, but it wouldn't enhance the game, and the bossy man said I can't make any big changes right now, anyway. Watching someone else play it really helps, so... thanks."

"Thanks for letting me help." I leaned over for a kiss.

"We have minor editing and cleanup of some code, plus updating the documentation and the player's guide before the game can be validated."

"And... what's that? Someone checks it?"

"Usually the publisher, but in our case, we're going

using a company to do it. It goes beyond Quality Control. It lets us know the game is up to standards and gives us an objective view of things like first time play experience, controller ergonomics, even security."

"Is that your last hurdle?"

"Pretty much. It won't stop us from premiering, but I want that rubber stamp that says we're ready."

"So then, GameBox is about securing funding? Distribution? Publishing?"

"Yes," he answered with a deep nod. "All the above. I need stability and cash flow to expand the team, to go from indie to a full time, big boy production. Not to mention I'd like to not drive an old Toyota and maybe move out of the attic of my studio."

The more he talked, the more my mind spun. And the more I had to remember what Steena told me—business. Not love.

But damn... if Parker Games could do all of that for him, it would be a win in both columns.

"So, let's say a flashy video game company offers to buy your game and slap their name on it. How big would that offer have to be for you to say yes?"

"There's not a number, India," he responded. "Seeing Galaxy Bros out there, knowing that me and four other guys worked our fingers to the bone and alienated loved ones and lost sleep and ate a shitload of pizza to make it happen? It doesn't get any better than that."

"I get it," I said, putting down the controller. The character ran in place on the screen. "Really, Malik. I love that you want to own your work, put it out yourself and you're willing to put the muscle behind it. You've done an amazing job. I'm proud of you."

I cupped his chin in my palm and brought his lips to

mine for a kiss. The game made a noise in the background that I was prepared to ignore, but Malik pulled back.

"You're about to die, baby. You need more charms to get to the next level."

"I think I'd rather play with you..."

"Nope." Malik picked up the controller and handed it back to me. "There's more I need you to see. Next level."

"I have to go through all the levels? I don't even know what I'm doing."

"I'll help you." He leaned into me, planting a trail of kisses up my neck. Chills chased his lips across my skin. "Start the game back up."

"And... how is this helping me?"

"Because if you stop, I stop. And from our conversation earlier, I know you don't want me to stop."

Malik scooted closer, then slid a hand up under my t-shirt, under the thin bra I wore. His fingers groped my breast, fingertips whispering over an already hardening nipple.

"Don't," I whined. "You know that makes me wet, Malik."

"Yep. I sure do."

"This is *not* fair."

"Yeah, it is. Choose your adventure. We playing, or what?" He asked, his thumbs coming to a standstill.

The realization of what he was about to put me through made me thump. I resumed the game. "Hell yes, we're playing."

"Good girl," he praised, nipping at my ear, his resuming caress of my breasts and teasing my nipples until they stood on end. "See that cloud right there?"

"Mmmmm...uh huh..."

"Jump up and tap it. There are extra charms in there. Those will get you to the next level."

I moved through the game as best I could for someone who didn't really know what I was doing and had to push through the distraction of being pleasured while playing.

"Any time you see something glowing, there's extra charms in there. Bank 'em, because you might need them."

"Really. Will those charms do more than rub on my titties?"

If this was how the game was going to be played, I was going to play the hell out of it. I spied his thickness in the crotch of his sweatpants. I didn't see us getting past the next level before we were naked and wrapped up in each other. The sooner we got to that point, the better.

"No. I will, though."

Malik slid off the couch and onto the floor in front of me, hooked his hands under the band of my leggings. I raised my hips so he could pull them off, then watched him toss them away.

"Pull your t-shirt off. I need access."

"Bra too?" I asked with a smirk, pulling my shirt off with one hand, and without my eyes leaving the screen. "It's just a sports bra."

"I'll handle that."

He pulled each breast from its cup and took his time bathing each nipple with his tongue before pulling the bra up so I could pull my arms through.

"Girl, you taste like brown sugar and honey," he said, adding a moan. "I've missed these right here."

"You can't be talking to me, Malik. I'm supposed to keep playing through this?"

"If you stop playing, I stop playing," he said, then spread my legs and lifted my thighs up and over his back. I hooked my ankles together behind him and slouched to bring myself closer to him. Trapping him. He seemed happy about it.

"This feels familiar…"

"Been trying not to get off all day, thinking about this moment right here."

He slid my panties to one side and gave one long, tortuously slow lick down my clit to my soaked pussy lips.

"Oh shit, oh shit, oh shit…"

The game made a noise… probably because I'd lost focus and my character was running in place into the wall when I leaned my head back and closed my eyes.

"You got to keep playing, baby," urged Malik. Then licked me again. And then again. And then again.

I hissed, trying to focus through my toes already curling. "Oh my God! Suck me. Please…"

"I'm getting to it. You still playing?"

"Only so you won't stop!"

"That's what I like to hear." Then he closed his mouth over my clit and sucked me so hard, my vision almost went black.

My hips involuntarily spasmed. I squealed through the pleasure, squeezing my thighs, winding my hips, doing all I could to concentrate on gems and charms when Malik was sucking my soul out of my body.

"Dammit, this isn't fair!"

My character fell short of a jump and landed in a ravine. I couldn't get them out and panicked. I smacked Malik on the top of his head. "Pause, please! I'm stuck!"

He released me and turned to glance at the screen. "Hit the back button three times. Get a running start, then jump again. You have to get over that canyon."

"There are coins down there, though."

"Look at your bank; you don't need to risk it for the coins. You have plenty to get you to the next level."

He walked me through the move again, and this time I made it over the canyon and past the pit.

"Whew," I sighed. Then I palmed his head and directed his attention back to me. "I have resumed play, but you have not."

"My bad, baby," he said, then went back to eating my pussy like it was dinner and he was a starving man. My breath caught in my throat just as he hit the spot, the tempo, the pressure that would make me climax. It was getting harder to keep playing.

But I couldn't let him stop.

He moaned in response, but his grasp on my thighs tightened. When two fingers slipped inside me, it sent me over the edge. For a moment, I thought the cheers and fireworks I heard were just in my brain, but I realized the sound was coming from the TV speakers.

I beat the level.

I tossed the controller to the floor and gripped his head in my hands, pulling him into me. I wound my hips, humping, grinding, riding the roughness of his tongue, screaming his name until I had milked every volt of electricity coursing through me.

Malik licked and kissed me until I stopped twitching. My legs were as heavy as tree limbs. I let them slip from his shoulders. When he was satisfied, he sat back, gazing up at me from between my legs.

"You did good for a first-time player."

"I had help." I leaned forward and kissed him. "You… are wearing essence of India."

"No other way I'd rather be," he responded quietly. "So you like the game?"

"Which one? Venus or Malik?"

He shrugged. "Either. Or both."

"That... was a fun game," I replied, out of breath, limp but satisfied. "I'll be ready for another level in a few minutes. It's your turn now."

CHAPTER TWELVE

india

DECEMBER 15, 2021

I marched into my office bright and early and on a mission. The sun hadn't yet risen, but Brew Bar was open, so I gripped a tall cup of coffee as I settled in behind my desk. I'd spent the weekend sneaking research about game platforms and publishers, watching documentaries, and had filled half of a notepad with questions.

An hour later, I heard soft singing and rustling outside my office.

"Evelyn?"

"Good morning!" She stepped into my office after a few moments. Her smile was as wide as it was bright. She was pretty in pink with a string of pearls around her neck.

"Did I miss an AKA holiday or y'all just wear pink and pearls all willy-nilly?"

She gave me a strong side eye. "If you're jealous I'm an AKA, just say that, Ms. Parker."

"Oh, no." I rolled my eyes. "Did your grandchildren teach you that?"

"They did." She grinned. Then frowned. "Did I use it right?"

"It's spicy. Make sure they teach you taking it as well as you dish it. Can you get Quinn for me?"

Her eyes popped open wide, and she removed her glasses. "Excuse me?"

"Get Quinn for me," I repeated, louder. "I need him in here. Immediately."

"Are *you* feeling spicy today? I can book you an ax throwing session instead."

I chuckled. "Not a bad idea, but I'm serious. I need to meet with him at his earliest convenience."

"Alright. I'll call him and tell him to come down."

Ten minutes later, a surly, middle-aged man in an ill-fitting suit stood in my doorway.

"India," he nearly growled. "You summoned me?"

I swiped my tongue across my teeth and sucked in a deep breath through my nose. Working with this man took more patience than I had stored up.

"I did. Leave the attitude at the door and have a seat."

He chose a seat and sat on the edge.

"Quinn. Relax. It's just me— the high schooler that you used to joke with behind my dad's back? I used to steal Jolly Ranchers from the candy bowl on your desk when you worked in marketing. By the way, apple Jolly Ranchers are still elite."

"I know who you used to be, India. I don't think I quite know who you are now. I figured you had decided to let me go. I don't want to waste any more time than necessary. And uhm..."

I saw a smile try to cross his lips. "Apple Jolly Ranchers

taste like Pine-Sol. I still separate them out. I remember that I used to save them for you."

"I have no plans to let you go unless you've decided to leave. Do you have an announcement?"

"Not at this time."

"Good. Listen...I understand where you're coming from. You've been here a long time, built up your organization under Bronson, had many accomplishments before I came along like the bratty lil sis, and stole the show. It's your job to identify new business ventures and bring new revenue streams to Parker.

"Then I swooped in with some pretty project called Service Kiosks and micromanaged the entire roll out. Suddenly, you're taking your orders from the boss' daughter when it should have been your concept to develop. I should have introduced the idea to you and let you cook, but I didn't. And I'm sorry, Quinn. I wanted you to know that."

Several rapid blinks and a long bout of silence later, he replied. "I... did not expect to hear that from you, India. Thank you for apologizing."

"I figured. And you're welcome."

I stood, walking around to the other side of the desk and sat in the seat across from him.

"I was so hell bent on proving myself. My dad casts a long shadow and even now, he's watching. I needed to show him I could do this job because I knew every corner of the business. Did you know I used to sweep floors at our first location?"

He stifled a laugh, then seemed to relax, sitting back. "I didn't know that. I can't imagine it, actually."

"What? Bronson Parker's Princess sweeping floors at nine years old? Oh, yes. You really think my hands never get dirty? You really thought I would take the CEO position and not work? Just sit here and look pretty, be the face of Parker? As much as Bronson spent on my degrees, my association memberships, you think all I have going for me is my looks, and not the breadth of experience he made sure I had before turning his company over to me?"

"The staff was bracing for you to be a figurehead, and we thought we would have to run the show when Bronson stepped down. We were surprised, I suppose, when you took the helm and did actual work. So, yes, that you would really just be the face of Parker occurred to me. But you've set me straight. So… you're not firing me?"

"Quite the opposite. I am giving you a project, something for you develop for us. Something that I can't take over and micromanage and steal your shine."

He sat forward, hands clasped. "I'm interested."

"What do you know about video games?" I asked.

"I know my son has to be dragged away from them, kicking and screaming, to have dinner, to do his homework, to shower. I know we spend a mint on games every month. I know holding them hostage is the only way to get what I want in my house."

His eyes narrowed. "Why? What are you cooking up?"

"Something to get consumers like your son to buy something from Parker."

I shared my thoughts, ideas and a thick folder of research on the concept of a gaming platform. For the first time, I saw a fire light up in Quinn's eyes.

"These platforms already exist, so we're not inventing anything. Just purposing the functionality for our purposes. We have a guide to go by— Steam, App stores, Oculus. I want to target an underserved niche. We establish ourselves as a place where developers publish their games to a platform that gives them control and let people know where to buy them."

"Hmmm." He crossed his arm, then tapped his chin with a stubby finger. "We already have a server farm. That's where we house our data. So...we'd sell video games? That's it?"

"Well, more like we *host* them. They live there. Players log in and play them there. I would first suggest an expansion of the server farm. We would need considerable bandwidth."

"It's quite the undertaking, India."

"But do-able. This could be the next kiosks for Parker. I need research, I need the upside, I need an objective eye and ear. To be clear, I want to make this happen so I need enthusiastic interest. I'm not looking for you to blow through it and reject it because it's my idea."

"I got it. I will give it the full court press. What's your timeline?"

"ASAP. There's a developer that is an... acquaintance. I want to put him on the platform and he's looking to launch soon."

"This could mean a significant investment. That would mean a vote from Bronson. It's an entirely new entity with its own infrastructure and mode of operation."

"I'm aware. I'm not afraid of my father. I have his every confidence. If the math works out in our favor, we've got ourselves a new enterprise."

I caught his watery blue-eyed stare. "Are we good, Quinn?"

He gave me a firm nod. "We're good, India. I'll get to work on this today."

CHAPTER THIRTEEN

December 17, 2021

I was nervous as *fuck* and had every reason to be. The day we had been preparing for at breakneck speed had arrived.

Corey, Rebekah, Brandon, and I spent the day before building our booth, setting up our tables, running power to the PCs and setting up the games. The booth was designed with spaces for multiple players to demo the game, so we had separate play areas to coordinate with wireless and Bluetooth connections.

"Yo, Malik." Brandon had disappeared earlier but came back into the exhibition hall with a drink carrier.

I heaved a sigh of relief. "Bro, please tell me that's coffee or liquid meth."

"As strong as it smells, it could qualify as both."

He handed me a tall cup of something dark and steamy. I took it, immediately sipping some off the top. It was hot and strong. I would need it.

"You look like shit," Brandon commented. "Did you get any sleep last night?"

I shook my head. I'd had to beg off of plans with India, because I didn't realize the time and manpower it would take to build and connect the booth. I got home around midnight and tried to crash, but my mind raced with possibilities and potential problems. I ended up back on the game until 4 AM, playing through each level just to be sure. I tossed and turned until it was time to meet the team.

"Wish I could say I did," I replied. "I'm pretty punchy. How about you?"

"Like a rock. Yesterday wore me out."

He sipped his coffee, then ran a palm over his close-cut fade. It was the easiest way to tame his curls, otherwise he sported a fro.

"You have time to look around at all?"

"I haven't wanted to leave the booth. Why?"

Brandon shrugged a shoulder, then nonchalantly sipped coffee. "Just saying. This 3D wrap that Rebekah designed is hot! It kicks the ass of any other booth out here. It's like we're the only game studio that took this shit seriously. Check it out."

I turned around, this time to do more than measure how far ahead or behind we were in our booth set up. It wasn't like other independent game studios were slacking — their booths were nice, slick, shiny, futuristic. They just weren't Galaxy Bros, and they didn't have Rebekah, who was a breakout in her graphic arts classes. She came highly recommended because she was a player who understood gamers and what attracted them. Most of what I wanted to do with additional financial footing was to put Rebekah to work full time, leading a team of graphic designers.

"You're right," I told Brandon. "The booth stands out.

It's taller, for one. I wanted to maximize space. If we can't be wider, be taller. I just hope the game lives up to the hype we've created."

"I'm not worried," he said, clapping me on the back. "We do good work. The game is good. Let's boot up and run through a couple of levels on each station. I want to make sure the wireless speed is good. No lags."

At 9 AM, the doors to the expo opened, and it was like a moth to a flame. The first hour was sheer madness, with attendees standing in lines for a chance to play the game, crowds gathering around their friends cheering and directing them from level to level, and a few men with stern faces in khakis with notepads and pens perusing the booth and the game.

I laughed to myself and eyed Brandon from across the booth. The money guys were never good at blending in. Most studios at this expo would look for them, though, and would welcome them with open arms.

Including me. By early afternoon, I had received my fair share of business cards from financial organizations, venture capitalists, and scouts for big game studios. And I'd been asked more than once if I was interested in selling the game.

My phone hummed a steady rhythm against my thigh most of the day. When the crowd thinned, I pulled it out and was greeted with several messages, but I only cared about the one from India, which had been sent an hour ago.

India: Hey, Lover :)

India: How is the expo?

Malik: Hey Lover. :) Nothing short of amazing

Malik: My pockets are full of business cards and the day is only half over.

India: Good! I hope you get a hit.

India: Really missed you yesterday. And last night.

India: And this morning.

Malik: Sensing a pattern...

Malik: I missed you, too. Wished I could have made it over to your place, but I was beat. Should have, though. I ended up not even sleeping.

India: See, we could have ended up not sleeping together. It doesn't always have to be games and sex. I just like lying next to you.

Malik: Noted. :)

Malik: How was your day yesterday? You didn't even text me to beg for adventures.

India: Didn't want to bother you. The day was good, though.

Malik: You are the highlight of my life right now. You never bother me. Tell me about your day.

India: Ha-ha. My business day is not text worthy.

India: I have a new project I'm working on though. Excited about it.

Malik: Can you talk about it yet?

There was a longer than usual pause. After a few beats, the dots resumed.

India: Not yet. Will talk about it when I can.

India: Pray for no push back. Tired of telling these people who I am.

Malik: They don't know the rule? When India Parker says move...

India: Only you obey that, baby :)

Malik: Bullshit.

Malik: India Parker doesn't take no for an answer. Keep reminding them that you're a beast.

Malik: Remind yourself while you're at it.

India: Thank you :)

A crowd surged through the front doors with a post-lunch burst of noise and energy, most of which headed right to the Galaxy Bros booth. I hopped to attention.

Malik: The booth is getting busy. Back to it. I'll see you tonight?

India: Can we celebrate with adventures?

Malik: ...absolutely

I closed the text app and locked it. India brought a smile to my lips so easily... but the face I saw as I slid my phone away wiped it away.

"Tony Clark," I called out, greeting the man that stood in front of me with a scowl on his lips and a deeply furrowed brow. He wore jeans and a polo and had a stack of brochures in one hand. "Are you lost? This doesn't seem like your kind of gig. Lot of thugs around here, as you call us."

He didn't acknowledge my greeting, at least not in

words. His eyes bounced around the booth from the background to the demo game to crowd standing around us.

"So, this is what you do?" He finally said, derision and judgment, riding every word. "India told me her ex worked for... *a tech company*. Did you lie to her about what you really do to get her to break up with me?"

"Actually..." I began slowly, about to tell him about himself, but decided to stay out of that minefield. "I run a tech company. Hines Tech provides several services. I write programs, bots, algorithms. We are also a game studio, and we produce video games. You literally secured the patent for the device that goes with our games."

"Yeah, yeah," he interrupted, his hand in the air. "I don't know what you have on India, but this? I knew something smelled fishy."

He laughed, pointing and waving his hands around. "I knew there had to be a reason for you to reconnect with India, and if you think you're going to scam her into funding your cute little games, I'm here to tell you it won't work. Unlike you, I have money and influence and the law on my side. I'll make sure you don't see a dime of Parker money."

"I haven't asked India for money or Parker for an investment—"

"Yet. You have a patented device that needs a retailer to sell it, don't you? Interesting how Parker is a retailer, and you fuck the CEO."

The mention of India made the hairs on the back of my neck stand on end. Out of the corner of my eye, I watched Brandon inch his way over to my end of the booth.

"I'm at GameBox to connect with organizations that want to do business with us. Unless you're here to offer partnership or sponsorship, I'll ask you to step aside so another person can view the game."

Tony's nostrils flared—a telltale sign I was getting under his skin.

Good.

"What I am is an attorney with a good grasp on trademark and intellectual property law. I represent a large number of software companies, who each have an expansive reach, so don't think I don't have connections."

"I don't know who you think you're threatening, but it's not me. I've asked you to step aside—"

"Hey, don't piss me off! You're out of your league, and I'm not just talking about games. You wouldn't want anyone to look into how closely your game resembles a very popular Nintendo game with a rock-solid copyright. Are you understanding me, or do I need to dumb it down for you?"

"I think it's time for you to be going, Tony." Brandon appeared next to me. "Been nice seeing you, but leave this booth, or I will call security."

Tony fumed, took one last look at the booth and stepped back, then stormed away. As soon as he was gone, I exhaled the breath I'd been holding.

"What's he doing here?" Brandon hissed, leaning in.

"Probably looking for new clients. Or someone to sue."

"Malik, I swear. I told you about this shit. A million IP lawyers in the phone book and you pick the one who used to date your girlfriend."

I turned away from him and pretended to be busy rolling wires. "B, I don't really want to hear this right now. It's not the time or the place to discuss this."

"You're risking our entire company on a pissing match over India Parker," he said, gripping my shoulder, turning me back around to face him. "If he fucks things up for us, that's all you're gonna hear."

I swore under my breath. I couldn't dig up any old IP or patent attorney—I had to hire *that* one, hanging on the unlikely hope that he'd bring me closer to India. And he hadn't even helped me with that.

"I think he wants to be a problem," I told Brandon. "But he's literally got nothing. I can handle him."

"You'd better. But if you can't, say the word and I'll rock him. Make it look like an accident."

I forced out a laugh. "It's not that serious. At worst, we make him a villain in the next game."

That made him chuckle. A little.

You're out of your league, and I'm not just talking games.

If I'd heard those words years ago, I probably would have agreed with them. But I was an older, wiser, new person years later. Maturity and accomplishment had given me the best sense of self.

I knew what league I belonged in and I wasn't out of place at all. And I wasn't talking about games, either.

It took almost as long to tear down the Galaxy Bros booth as it did to set it up. The team tried to dismiss me, but I wouldn't leave them to do the work alone, so we all dragged ourselves out of the convention center late that evening.

I pulled out my phone to text India as I ducked behind the wheel of my car.

Malik: Hey Lover :) Done for the day

India: Hey Lover. :)

India: Just now? I thought I worked hard.

Malik: And you do. Heading home.

India: Drinks with Steena. She says hi.

Good, I thought. I wouldn't feel guilty about blowing her off another night if she was already out.

Malik: Don't leave Steena for me. Have fun.

India: Steena has plans. Thought we did too?

Malik: Beat. Sorry, baby. I'm just going to grab something quick to eat and crash.

India: I'll bring you dinner. And crash with you.

India: You're about to argue and I want you to rest your thumbs. See you in a few.

I paused mid text, about to do exactly what she called me out for. I smiled to myself and tossed the phone into the bag next to me.

I'd been drifting in and out of sleep for a while until the sun poked me awake. I heard breathing that wasn't mine and felt the weight of someone else in the bed. There was nothing like waking up next to India in the morning.

She was curled up on her side and laying on my arm with her back to me. It took me a few nights before I realized that she always brought a canvas bag with a few products, that long nightshirt she liked to wear and her headscarf. I loved her in her scarf and nightshirt.

We were so comfortably moving back to old habits and

routines. It was the rhythm of our relationship that I missed. Morning coffee together and late-night talks... and India making sure I had at least one good meal. Seven years of pain and growth, hardship and triumph changes a person, for sure, but the foundation we had built was still there.

It was still love.

She stirred when I ran my palm down her body, over her thighs. When I found the hem of her nightshirt, I snaked a hand up under it and cupped the first round cheek I could get my hands on.

"Mmmph. What are you doing?" She rolled over to face me and tossed a leg over mine. Then laid her head on my shoulder and leaned in to kiss the skin on my chest.

"Finding a gentle way to wake you up to play with me."

My fingers made their way to the warmth between her thighs again. I lightly stroked her, feeling her wetness build and gather on my fingertips.

She slid a palm down my body until she found me-rigid, waiting, wanting. We fed off of each other, quietly stroking, playing, kissing, whispering, giggling...until the pressure and the desire to be infinitely closer to her was overwhelming.

I didn't expect anyone to come to the studio, especially the week before Christmas, but since we were so close to publication, someone could decide to come in early and get some work done while it was quiet. I hoped Brandon had told the team to roll in a little late today, but I'd forgotten to check.

I would have to take my chances because I needed to be inside her.

I rolled over to pull open a drawer next to the bed and

retrieve a strip of condoms. I tore off one and tossed the rest back into the drawer.

When I rolled back over, I was greeted with a smug grin. "Do men keep a stash of condoms around in case you get to fuck? Or do you buy them because you plan to fuck?"

"I bought them, hoping to fuck." I laughed as I rolled the latex on. Then I got out of bed and stood up. I offered a hand to India. "Come here."

"I'm warm," India whined. "Where we going?"

"Right here. Adventure time." I hiked a brow at her. She hopped up then and scrambled out of bed to stand next to me. "Stop playing. You know which way I want you to be."

She smirked and turned around, pulling her nightshirt off.

"Who said I wanted you to do that? You unwrap other people's presents?"

"You move too slow."

"You are impatient."

I edged up behind her, moving closer until skin meshed into skin and there wasn't a sliver of light between us. I slid my hands around her waist, then up to cup her round, heavy breasts in my hand. I felt myself growing harder as soon as I touched her, heard her gasp, felt the nubs tighten under my fingers.

I began a slow grind up against her, moving between her cheeks. She matched my rhythm and ground back against me.

"Oh, I like that," I whispered in her ear. 'Throw that ass back."

She giggled... until I moved one hand to my favorite spot and leaned into her, bending her forward over the bed.

"Ohhh yes. I can't wait."

She reached forward, legs spread, gripping the sheets

with both hands for leverage. I had to pause for just a moment to take in the view of her ample ass staring up at me. India wiggled and whimpered, so I had to cut the appreciation short.

Besides, I couldn't wait another second to enter her. Pushing in, pulling out, then pushing in further, over and over again and again, until I was buried inside her and the condom was slick with her wetness.

"Tell me how you want this, baby. Nice and slow, or—"

"No," she whimpered, winding her hips and rolling her body against mine. "I need it hard. Fuck me hard."

"If I fuck you hard, I want my neighbors to hear you coming."

She laughed. "Try to shut me up."

At her urging, I increased speed and pumped my hips against hers with vigor. As promised, her cries were full throated, accompanied by the lusty sounds of our thighs clapping together. I gripped her waist, digging my thumbs into her skin so hard I left marks.

I felt myself approaching the crest and, as usual, I wasn't trying to go over the edge alone. "Baby, I want to come."

"I'm close!" She gasped. "Keep...shit! Right there, don't stop!"

"You comin'? I'm coming with you."

"Yes! Yes! Fuck yes!"

A violent series of convulsive squeezes gripped me. I let myself go, the relief nearly making my eyes roll back in my head.

I hissed, throwing my head back, basking in release. I felt India go limp and held onto her so she didn't fall over. I pulled out, then guided her back up on to the bed. She got up there on all fours, then collapsed into the pillows.

I laid next to her, grabbed her face and kissed her hard.

"I'm not saying this because we just finished fucking... but I really missed you."

"I *am* saying I missed you because we just finished fucking. I am done with my *putting up with raggedy dick* era. I can't go back."

"I pray you never have raggedy dick ever again."

"Let's touch and agree."

She reached over to lay a hand on my bicep and squeezed. We laid together under the overhead fan and let it dry our sweat.

"I've worked up an appetite. Are you feeding me?"

"Uhm..." I stretched, laughing at the pop of bones and muscles. "Unless we're eating last night's leftovers, we have to go out. We can walk down to West End for breakfast. Or, if you don't have time, we can order—"

She leaned over and kissed me, shutting me up. "I'm meeting Steena to finish Christmas shopping. She needs a dress for her family's holiday cocktail party. And I still have to pick up a gift for my dad's birthday party."

She stopped talking, then sat up. I knew what was coming and tried to head it off.

"India, I don't think—"

"You should come! It's just a birthday party. He'd love to see you."

"Bronson would not *love* to see me. He would tolerate seeing me because he loves you."

"I'm being serious."

"So am I. You really want to bring me around your parents and your family and... everybody? After I've been gone for so long?"

"Yeah," she replied after a thoughtful pause. "You'll have to see them, eventually."

"You're going to just show up at a family party with some guy—"

"They know you, Malik."

"— right after you stopped dating a prominent attorney—"

"Who was sleeping with at least one other person while he was sleeping with me."

I shrugged. I couldn't define how it felt to be invited to a family gathering at the Parker home. In a different lifetime, Bronson and Junie were nice enough to me, but I always sensed *not good enough* undertones from them. I was not in a hurry to step back into wondering if they all would rather she date a rich, influential billionaire.

She frowned. "I understand if you're uncomfortable, or if you think it's too early. I'd love for you to come, but you don't have to."

"So... who all gon' be there?" I asked. "Do I have to dress up?"

"Steena. My dad's friends. Neighbors. Staff at Parker. It's like any other party. Grab a drink, get lost in the crowd. They get real loose and much friendlier once the bar opens."

I groaned, memories of Bronson's birthday parties rushing back like a wave. "I remember Bronson making us do the Electric Slide at 3 AM."

"In his dress socks, jacket off, without spilling his whiskey," India finished, laughing. "I really want you to come. It'll be the first year since I took over Parker. I want to have someone in my corner."

"And I want to be that person. I want you to have fun, though. Not be on the defensive about me with your family. I can stand on my own two feet."

"Malik, you can stand wherever you want on your own two feet. Just let me stand beside you. Please?"

"Alright, I'll go." I poked my finger at the fat bottom lip that stuck out. Then cupped her cheek to bring her lips back to mine. "For you. I'll be your arm candy."

"You aren't my arm candy. You are... a different kind of candy," she said. Then ran her tongue up the outside of my ear. Goosebumps and chills ran down my body. "But still very lickable."

I squeezed the flesh in my palm. "Stop playing with me, woman. What time are you heading out to meet Steena?"

"Not until much later," she answered. "I'm yours until then. If you want me."

"If I want you? If I have you again, I'm not letting you go."

india

I was so giddy about sitting my freshly redecorated office that I could hardly stand myself. All it took was a little paint, new carpet, and a whole new suite of furniture to make the space look like it belonged to me.

When the interior decorators came by to present their ideas for an updated executive office space, I frowned at most of the options. They were a dull gray, beige and white motif or a dark and moody black and mahogany wood affair. Toward the back of the catalog, I found a room that fit me well.

"That. I like that."

I'd replaced my father's behemoth desk and oversized leather executive chair with a more feminine style desk with a glass top and a silver metallic finish. The guest chairs and meeting table complemented the set so well. I completed the look with curated art and photos of my father, myself, and my family around the room.

I'd never put out photos of Tony at the office. Even if we weren't an actual couple, we were supposed to be, and had fooled enough people that most assumed we were Atlanta's next power couple. I refused to post up a photo of him like he was my man.

But I couldn't wait to set out photos of me and Malik.

"Isn't it funny that a few weeks ago, we couldn't get you to work out of this office?" Evelyn joked when she arrived for our weekly meeting. "Now it's like pulling teeth to get you to meet anywhere but in here."

"That's what you and Steena get for harassing me to work up here. It turned out great, didn't it?"

"Very nice." She nodded her approval. "And don't tell Bronson, but I like this much better than his old office."

"Junie already told him that it looked like a malt liquor commercial was shot in here."

We had a good, long belly laugh, then settled down to business, popping open our calendars and notepads to begin our meeting.

"So, I need to set a meeting to review fourth quarter performance. I know we won't have numbers until at least the second week in January." I poked a fingernail between my teeth and studied the calendar. "Then we run up on the Martin Luther King Jr. holiday."

Mmhmm," Evelyn hummed. Her glasses were perched on the ends of her nose and her fingers flew across the thin keyboard attached to her iPad. I marveled at how quickly she had picked up new technology since I came aboard. She loved the transportable device, and it kept her connected even when she wasn't at her desk. "They'll be concentrating on holiday sales before that anyway, so the numbers are always late—"

The door to my office flew open so fast, I was surprised it stayed on its hinges.

"Oh, my Lord!" Evelyn yelped, rising quickly from her seat as if she could pounce on whoever barged into my office.

The irritation that it was Tony, someone I did not want to see, mitigated the momentary relief that it was only Tony and not an intruder. He had only made a few appearances at Parker during our relationship. I didn't even know how he'd made his way into my office.

Then again, it wasn't like I had made a companywide announcement that we had broken up. The front desk and security personnel knew him and probably let him up.

"Tony," I greeted him, refusing to stand just because he had entered the room. "This is a surprise. What are you doing here?"

"We need to talk."

"We have nothing to talk about. I'm in a meeting and you're being rude. Unless it's an emergency and business related, it's going to have to wait."

"It's business related and depending on what you've been doing with your money, it could be an emergency. Do you know what your boyfriend does for a living?"

Evelyn glanced from me to Tony and back. "I... I'm sorry, dear. I thought you—"

"Tony and I are no longer together, as of weeks ago," I explained. "He decided to seek greener, and I assume younger pastures, so I'm not sure why he's here in my office asking about a man I've been spending time with."

"Answer me. Do you know what that guy does for a living?"

I pushed out a loud sigh. "Evelyn—"

"I'll get ghost. Excuse me." She gathered her things and scurried from the room, closing the door behind her.

I gestured for Tony to take a seat. He did so, flapping a thin manila folder down on the desk.

"I cannot believe you busted into my office on some jealousy shit when you were the one fucking some chick in your office when you were supposed to be at a dinner for me. What do you want? And why are you asking about Malik?"

"I don't think you know what he really does for a living. Do you?"

I knew exactly what Tony thought of Malik when they faced off at my front door. That Tony thought Malik was below him was obvious.

"He runs a technology studio that does a number of things that go over my head, but his passion is to write and publish video games for Black gamers."

"He—" Tony's mouth snapped shut. I'd never seen him speechless before. He seemed dumbfounded and confused for longer than a few seconds. Then he snapped back. "He makes video games, India. Do you hear yourself? Are you okay with that?"

"What is there to be okay with? He's talented and the games he creates are fun. I don't understand why we are still having this conversation after you told me you don't want to be my fake boyfriend."

"This is not about us—"

"Sure, it isn't."

"It's about protecting you from a potential scammer. A predator."

I nearly choked on my laughter. "A predator? I have known Malik since college. If he was going to prey on me, it would have been long before now."

"This guy is a loser with no money."

He flipped open the folder and laid out pages of an extensive background check. The thought of even looking at those pages made me feel physically ill.

I pushed the pages across the desk, away from me.

He pushed them back toward me. "Look at this. Look at who he is!"

"I know who he is, Tony. Are you so unhinged that you ran a background check on my ex-boyfriend? But you're *not* jealous and *not* bothered that you saw us that morning, right?"

"India, just look—"

"I don't want to. And I don't need to. Beyond these pieces of paper—" I shuffled them together and dropped them back into the folder. "There is a real person we're talking about here. There's not a thing in this folder that will surprise me. I know him."

"Then you know his company needs money to keep publishing games."

"Most companies need funds to stay afloat. It's not a novel concept, considering the clients you work with. Why do you care?"

"Because you need to think about why he would reconnect with you right now. I was at this tech expo downtown —GameBox? I ran into your boy and his crew out there in his booth."

"He sent me pictures. I think it turned out great."

"You are *not* listening to me," said Tony, seething through his tight jaw and biting out his words. "It's not like he's backed by a big organization— Microsoft, X-Box, EA Games. If he doesn't get funding, no more games. No more games means no more company, and he's out on his ass and living on your couch. How do you know he doesn't live in his car? Have you ever been to his place?"

My cheeks flushed at the mention of Malik's place. The casual, laid back evenings. The slow, lazy mornings. The unique way he helped me learn the game. The spine-tingling orgasms. *Plural.*

"I've been to the studio where the games are developed. I've played a prototype of the new game. I've seen the device that's now patented. I've spent meaningful time at his home."

I caught his eye and lowered the register of my voice, my head tilted to the side. "Doing... *meaningful* things."

I knew exactly what I was doing, and Tony might act like an idiot, but he wasn't one. I wasn't trying to make him jealous; he was already there.

I was having fun fucking with him, though.

"I get that you're concerned, but it's unfounded. I know what Malik does. I know the financial status of Hines Tech. I know his goals and his dreams. The point of showing the games at GameBox was to put him in the path of people who can fund the studio. If you cared about your client at all, you'd know this. He hasn't asked me for a thin dime-"

"Yet."

"But if he did," I continued, "it would be up to me to grant or deny that request. And I'd do so with my eyes wide open and industry research backing my decision. I'm not sure if three years of fake dating me taught you anything, Tony, but I'm actually quite business savvy. I can forward a few articles if you need reference points."

"I didn't call you a moron, India." Tony rolled his eyes, as he always did when I asserted my place in the business world. I knew what I was doing, but he rarely acknowledged it. "Mark my words— this guy is going to eventually ask you for money. I'm sure I'll see it in the Chronicle when Parker makes a mysterious investment into a small Atlanta based Black owned tech company."

"Like I said, it would be my decision if we did. And that is none of your business. I think you're done, here. I have meetings to get to."

He stood and slid the folder toward me again. "Check out that info. Hire a good lawyer," he advised, before turning to leave my office.

After he left, Evelyn came back, iPad and keyboard tucked into the crook of her elbow. "What on earth was that about? I've never seen a person so worked up before."

I waved a hand in the air. "Never mind him. Could you send a note to the front desk and security that Tony Clark is no longer permitted in the building? I don't want him in my office ever again."

"Of course, right away. But what's the tea on what happened with that young man? I thought you and he were headed down the aisle."

I exhaled a relieved breath, dropping into my chair with the bottle of water I'd opened. "It's kind of a long story."

"My favorite kind of story," she replied.

I filled Evelyn in, leaving out a few parts I didn't want to get around Parker. My father trusted her, and I liked her a lot, but the less I said out loud, the better. She shook her head, sucked her teeth, folded and unfolded her arms throughout the story.

"Well, good riddance," she declared, when I'd told her there would be no wedding bells, and that was that.

"Indeed. The funny thing is... he broke up with me. Why does he keep coming around?"

"Oh, you know what this is, child. He sees you happy, moving on— and so quickly— and now he's having second thoughts about what he gave up. He fumbled an entire closet full of luxury bags when he let you catch him stepping out."

"Oooh, Evelyn! That was a good one! Who taught you that one?"

"I made that one up myself," she replied, beaming. "I'm pretty proud of it."

"You should be. Getting spicier by the day!" I tapped her on the arm and winked. "Listen...Christmas is in two days. The building is empty. Let's play hooky and pick this up next week."

"I've got 99 things I'd rather be doing and work ain't one!"

"Evelyn..." I shook my head at her. "Your grandchildren are on punishment. Go pack up your desk. I'll get a car for you."

She nodded and pulled the door shut behind her. I arranged a black car Uber for Evelyn, then powered down my laptop, remove my phones from their chargers, and pack my work bag. I eyed the folder that Tony had left on the desk. I contemplated leaving it, but I didn't want anyone to find it.

There was nothing in that folder that would be a surprise to me, but the part of my business savvy brain that wanted to ensure my due diligence was properly executed niggled at me.

You should at least look at it, since Tony went through the trouble to run the report. Make sure you know what you know.

"It just makes business sense," I told myself, stuffing the folder into my bag, sliding my slim laptop in beside it.

"I'm late, I'm late, I'm late!"

I'd been spending so much time with Malik— late nights and early mornings and despite being a regular at boot camp workouts, the vigorous sexual activity lately was wearing me out. Not that I was complaining, but I was nearly delirious when I got home. I laid down for a nap after work, overslept, and now I was way behind in getting ready for the annual holiday cocktail party at Steena's parent's house.

I rushed through a shower, plugged in my curling iron and set out my skincare and makeup to run through my routine.

"Hey, Siri?" I called out.

"Hmmm?" My phone's AI assistant replied.

"Dial Malik."

The line rang and just as I thought it was going to roll to voicemail, Malik picked up.

"Hey!" He answered, breathless. "Almost missed you."

I giggled, pulling the brow pencil away from my face before I stabbed myself in the eye. "Uh...hey? Just... *hey*?"

"Hey, lover. That better?"

"Much." I smiled, then answered back. "Hey, lover. Why do you sound out of breath? What are y'all doing over there?"

"I tried to slide down the hall to pick up your call before voicemail got it. It turns out I'm not 27 anymore."

I heard him huff and drop into his desk chair. I could tell by the faint squeaks in the background.

"When are you going to oil that chair?"

"Never. It keeps the team on their toes. Makes them think I'm coming for them. What uh... what's up? You getting ready for your party?"

"Yeah." I rifled through my makeup case for my favorite

NAKED eye shadow pallet. "Steena is on her way to pick me up and I'm running way behind. I'm finishing my makeup before I get dressed. Otherwise, I get makeup all over everything."

"See, you've made the mistake of telling me you don't have any clothes on," he said, his tone low, almost growling into the speaker. "I feel an adventure coming on..."

I snorted. "I wish I had time. So, I got a visitor at Parker today. Is there anything need to tell me?"

"There's a lot I need to tell you, specifically how I feel about you not having any clothes on. But it sounds like you're trying to trap me in something. What do I need to tell you?"

"That you saw Tony at GameBox Expo."

"Oh." Malik pushed out a few unenthused chuckles. "Yeah, we saw him out there, probably trolling for clients."

"Well, what happened? What did he say to you?"

"He checked out the booth, looked down his nose at us, said something about being nice to him or he had connections that would make trouble for us."

"What kind of trouble?"

"Something about how the characters in Galaxy Bros look enough like another game's main characters that he could work up a copyright infringement suit. You've been around for most of the game creation. You know good and well we didn't copy anybody's game to make ours."

"Yeah, I know. I just..." I sighed, pressing my palms into the cool countertop. Tony made me unreasonably nervous. "You're sure he doesn't have anything in his back pocket that he could use to hurt you?"

"Can't think of anything, really," he said. "We lie low. We just write games, you know? What was he doing at your office?"

"He thought you had lied to me about the games, about Hines Tech. He was hoping to catch me before I fell into your trap."

"Too late. You're deep in the trap, baby."

I grinned, filling in the space between my brow and eye liner with a lush shade called Frisk. It was close to nude but added some sparkle. "Listen, Tony's manic right now. He's not used to not getting what he wants. I need to make sure you're alright, that he didn't say anything to you he shouldn't have said."

"And if he did? What would you do about it?"

"Well, I could—"

"Nothing," he cut in. "Baby, let that man be jealous. Let him marinate in it—matter of fact, I hope he can't stop thinking about how good we must be together. I hope he can't stop wondering if I like how you taste. If I love your scent. I hope he remembers how soft your skin feels, and he hates how well you fit in my arms. He gave up all of that and I've got it now, and we're just gonna let that dude be mad about it."

"Damn. Why do I have plans tonight?" Malik replied with an evil laugh. I fished through my Fenty lip color collection, selecting a deep wine shade. "So, what are the Hines boys doing tonight?"

"Brandon and his fiancée have dinner with her folks. I'm hanging out here. Might try to call my dad— I haven't talked to him in a minute. He's got an appointment coming up in January, so we need to make plans to get him to Atlanta to check in."

"Tell Cliff I said hello, if you reach him."

"I will. He'll be happy to hear that you're back in my life. I can say that, right? That you're back in my life?"

"Try to get rid of me, Malik Hines."

"So, uh… you have this thing with Steen tonight. And tomorrow is Christmas Eve, but I was hoping to see you—"

"Yes!" I answered, a little too quickly. "Whatever you want to do. I'd love to wake up next to you on Christmas morning."

I'd cleared the evening with the sole purpose of hinting that we should get together. We would both be with our families for Christmas, so an evening with Malik would be the perfect prelude.

"Bet on that. Plans already in motion." I heard the smile in his tone. "I'll try not to text you what I'm thinking about, knowing you're not dressed. Do you have *anything* on? Or are you in the bathroom just gloriously naked, water dripping off of your titties, ass sitting high and round, everything just… thingin'?"

"I'm not telling unless you promise to tell me what you're thinking about."

"Nah. It'll keep until tomorrow."

"What happened to *when India Parker says move?*"

"Have fun tonight. I'll let you know what's up tomorrow and what time to be ready. Then we'll bring it back to your place for Netflix and Chill. Heavy on the chill and you know what that means."

"Not chillin', that's for damn sure."

I heard a beep, and Steena's face and phone number rolled across the screen. "Shit, I gotta go. I'm not ready yet and Steena is going to be pissed."

I picked up Steen's call, answering with, "Don't hate me."

"I already know your ass has been wasting time, caking with that man."

"Guilty. I fell asleep and I'm rushing around. You're going to have to come up for a few minutes."

"Don't let that sexy geek get you on my bad side," said Steena, the sound of road noise and raucous rap music in the background.

"I need you to zip me into this pantsuit, anyway. We can pre-game with some wine or something."

"Deal, I guess." she replied. I could always ply her with drinks. "See you in a minute."

CHAPTER FIFTEEN

DECEMBER **24, 2021**

"Whoa. You going to a wedding or something?"

Rebekah was the first to notice me coming down the stairs. Her low gasp made the others turn to see what she was gawking at. I descended the stairs in one of two new suits I'd purchased.

"Dinner date," I answered, pausing on the bottom step to model my fit. "You like? How I look?"

"Sharp, man. Hold up though." Corey rushed toward me to adjust the collar of my jacket, make sure my lapels were flat and the cuffs of my dress shirt were pulled. The matte black 'H' cuff links I'd inherited from my father winked from under my sleeve.

Brandon had arranged an afternoon celebration for the team to commemorate major code completion on Galaxy Bros: Venus and a successful day at GameBox. We had uploaded a mobile version of the game to app stores and the team was eating, drinking and anxiously and incessantly checking download numbers.

It was now on me to secure a deal to retail the Game Stick and to host our suite of games. The pressure weighed heavily on my shoulders... but it was the holidays and I promised myself that I'd take time off to enjoy having India back in my life.

I'd made a reservation at Canoe, an upscale southern fare restaurant in an elegant garden setting overlooking the Chattahoochee River. I couldn't give her the star-studded parties and expensive designer looks that Tony was known for, but knowing India meant knowing none of that turned her head. It burned me he'd wasted years of her time and hadn't learned that basic fact about her. He was so close.

But she was mine now, back where she belonged. Tony could throw all the tantrums he wanted. I would not be sharing her affection.

"Alright, folks. I'm out. I don't want anyone in here tomorrow—the studio is closed. And just so nobody will be gossiping. I will not be back this evening." I moved to the door to pick up my heavy wool coat and an overnight bag I'd packed. "B, see you at dinner tomorrow. Be safe, y'all."

Nobody paid attention to me as I pulled open the door and stepped outside. Twenty minutes later, India's wreath-laden front door swung open before I could knock, and I was blown over at the vision that stood in the doorway.

Sheer sleeves ran the length of her arms, accenting the body hugging black and gold print dress that clung to her shape like a man hanging off a ledge. Suede pumps dyed to match the color of her dress and gold glittering jewelry finished the look.

A growl rolled through my chest as I stepped inside. She laughed as I crowded her in her foyer, sliding my arms around her waist, digging my nose into her neck and planting loud, wet kisses across her shoulder.

"You smell amazing," I muttered, sucking in a warm, spicy fragrance. "What is that? I want to buy you a gallon of it."

"It's nothing fancy. Hypnotic Poison by Dior. You like it?"

"Might be my new favorite thing." I released her, slowly and reluctantly. "Are you ready, or do you have twenty more minutes of prep?"

"I just need to change over my evening bag from last night. Come in, have a seat for a minute."

I headed for the living room, knowing that a minute could mean a half hour. I settled in on the couch where India's work bag had been haphazardly tossed on the cushion. I picked up one of the straps to move it, but it was heavy on one side and toppled over, spilling the contents out on the cushion.

"Oop...shit," I mumbled, grabbing everything before it slid anywhere, particularly the pages that had come almost completely out of the folder. I figured most of her work would be confidential, so I was trying not to glance at the pages... until I saw my name.

Malik Roydell Hines. DOB 9/24/86.

I paused, fighting with myself- keep reading, or put it away?

Put it away, man. That's not your stuff, not your business.

It's about me. That makes it my business.

I scanned the page quickly, simultaneously horrified and intrigued by the background report provided to India. I knew me, my history and my background- there would be nothing surprising or salacious on that report.

India knew me, too. Why did she run a background report instead of just asking?

Was she trying to protect her business, which I could understand... or herself? The latter threatened to stab me in the heart.

Maybe she still didn't trust that I had the best intentions when I reached out to her after so many years apart. She claimed to not hold any malice about how we broke up, but a smart woman would be wary of a man coming back around seven years later. Particularly a man in my position, pursuing a woman in hers.

I returned her belongings to the state I found them. I scooted the pages back into the folder and slid it back into her bag, followed by her laptop, a pair of wireless earbuds, and a small clear plastic case that held pens, highlighters, and an extra pair of drugstore readers. I set the bag back on the cushion next to me, then got up and returned to the foyer, where I couldn't find more things to make me question whether India was giving us a fair shake.

"Time's wasting," I called down the hall. "In about thirty seconds, I'm coming in there to take that dress off of you. I don't mind Door Dashing some McDonald's or whatever—"

"Don't tempt me," she said, chuckling as she walked out of her bedroom, a velvet bag under her arm. She stopped to open a door, pulled out a floor length coat and handed it to me. "Help, please."

"I'm serious," I said, only half joking as she turned around so I could help her put the heavy wool coat on. "I can be out of this suit in like... fifteen seconds."

"Good to know," she replied, then turned and stepped close, pushing her body against mine. "I bought this dress specifically go to dinner tonight and I'm excited to do something with you that requires us to stand up."

"We can fuck standing up, you know." I winked as I teased her, then brushed my lips across hers. "Last chance."

"Let's go, Malik. Before I take you up on that."

Being able to take India to a nice place, tell her to order whatever she'd like, have as many glasses of wine as she wanted to drink, and however many desserts she wanted to share showed me how far I'd come from the man she used to know.

Back in the day, a nice night on me meant Longhorn Steakhouse, which wasn't bad, but it wasn't New York Prime, or Canoe, tonight's venue. To India's credit, she never turned up her nose at what I could afford, but my preconceived notions about being able to provide, to love her the way she should be loved, kept me from assuring myself that I was the man she needed.

I slid my credit card into the payment folder and scowled across the table when she suggested she leave the tip. "I got this. Your job tonight is to relax and let me take care of you."

"Well, alright then," she said, sending me a sultry smile before she brought a glass to her lips and a sip of rich wine disappeared into her mouth. "This is a beautiful restaurant. The patio view must be amazing in the summer." She nodded to the pearl lights strung along each side of the walkway down to the river and around the covered patio.

I preferred the view of India across the table. I spent the

evening admiring the cut of her dress, how it showcased her full figure. My mind was busy writing adventures where I could explore the scented valley between her breasts and work my way down her body from there.

The server returned with the folder and my card. I slid it back into my wallet and sent a meaningful stare in her direction. "Let's get out of here. We have an appointment to... *chill*. All night."

She finished her wine and nodded. "I am ready for all of that."

I'd parked in a corner of the parking lot, since the restaurant had been packed when we arrived. We'd taken our time, and the crowd had thinned considerably, leaving my car by itself in the dark. Instead of waiting for me to drive the car around, India insisted on walking with me.

We crossed the lot, hands clasped, and reached the car in a few minutes. I used the key fob to unlock the doors and walked India around to the passenger side.

But she opened the back door and ducked into the seat.

"India," I called after her, bending to see her in the darkness of the backseat. "What are you doing? You looking for something?"

"Looking for you. Come here."

She reached out and grabbed my lapel, pulling me in with her. We tussled for room and space before I could close the door, and as soon as we were shrouded in darkness, India's fingers were at my waist, fumbling with my belt buckle and then my zipper.

"What is happ—"

"Shhhhh..."

Nimble fingers groped my length through my briefs. Her lips found mine, and I gave in to the warmth of her mouth and the aggressive swirl of her tongue. She moaned and pressed herself up against me.

Before I realized what was happening, she had pulled my dick out and was stroking me from base to tip and back—slow, sensuous strokes that drove me out of my mind in the best way.

"I have been thinking about this all night," she whispered, so close to my ear that the hairs stood. "When I saw where we were parked, I wrote a game of my own."

"This game might get us arrested," I said. "Go 'head though. I like where you're going with it."

I let my legs fall open to give her room and put my hands to work, pulling off her coat so I could get to the zipper at the back of her dress. Once the skintight body con material was loose enough, I dipped a hand into the bodice to cup a breast. Her nipples were rock hard in my palm and from the sounds she made when I flicked my thumb across the hardened nub, she liked it.

"You know why your Toyota is better than my BMW?" She asked in a breathless whisper that I barely heard, mostly because it took all my brain power to concentrate on her hands.

"I feel like you're going to tell me."

She got on her knees, then kicked a leg over my lap and sat on my thighs. "I can't do this in my backseat," she said, laughing.

The hem of her dress had already ridden so far up that her thick, luscious thighs were on display. I rubbed on them, loving the sensation of supple skin before I tucked a finger under the band of her panties. I found her clit and stroked her, matching the rhythm she was using on me.

She whimpered, writhing. The sounds she made in the throes of passion were always an aphrodisiac to me. Over the years, all I needed to get going was to recall the noises she made when she was on the verge of climax.

Her palms were giving me the best hand job I'd probably ever had- tight, rhythmic, warm, wet. My hips began to undulate, moving myself into and out of her grasp. She rocked her body against mine, hands moving more quickly, low moans reaching my ear and sending me higher.

"I'm about to come."

India moved from my lap to the floor between my legs and took me into her mouth. It was so quick and unexpected that I erupted immediately, arching against the seat, rocking the car and failing to keep the sounds of my orgasm quiet.

"Now who's getting us arrested?" India whispered, giggling.

"I was trying not to come first." I was sweating through my suit and out of breath like I'd just run a mile.

"You can owe me."

I moved over and pulled her onto the seat next to me, then edged her back. "Thing is, I don't like owing people. Get comfortable."

I stifled her giggle when I kissed her while I groped for the band of her panties. When I had pulled them down far enough, she kicked them off. I sat back... then dove between her open thighs.

I aimed for her clit, alternating flicks of my tongue and long, hard, rhythmic sucks until she cupped my head in her hands and bucked her hips into my face. The sounds of her orgasm set me up for another round, but I was already worried that we were about to be discovered.

A few quiet moments later, we had managed to sit upright in the backseat, leaning against one another and sharing soft kisses.

I drew an arm around her and kissed her temple. "So…" I sniffed. "The fuck was that about?"

"Mid-life crisis?" She suggested. Then laughed. "Something I always wanted to do. With someone I always wanted to do that with."

"I can't say I never thought about it."

India tipped her head up so she could see me. She reached up to caress my cheek, then pressed her lips to mine. "I had a wonderful time tonight. Dinner and wine and dessert and the company and conversation were everything. But I would have been fine eating pizza and playing games."

"I know. And we've had that evening. I wanted to treat you to a nice night out because I can give that to you now."

"I like that you've always been hyper focused on me getting what I deserve. And I don't disagree. It's just…"

She sat up, moving to face me.

"There's a lot of pressure to be me. So much on my shoulders, on my mind, in my realm of responsibility. All I really want is to be with someone that lets me shed all of that, that lets me be the woman that loves a night where I don't have to put on a couture dress and wear heels and smile for the public. Who pushes the designer bags and shoes to the back of the closet and willingly wears Crocs to the mall."

"Crocs?" I repeated.

"Steena hates them, and I love irritating her by wearing them in public."

"I followed you online for years. You're in the spotlight a lot. You're not worried about being caught in a parking lot doing unholy things in the backseat of a car with an unknown man?"

"Honestly? Not really," she said, surprising me with her

response. "I had a ball in the backseat of this car. The woman I am right now is the woman you should be working to deserve. I promise she is easier to please than India Parker, CEO."

"So... what does this woman I'm with want right now?"

"For you to drive us home so we can undress each other and fuck until Christmas morning."

My dick throbbed in response.

We adjusted our clothing and, nearly an hour after we'd first attempted to leave the restaurant, climbed into the front seat. As soon as the satellite radio kicked in, India tuned to LL Cool J's *Rock the Bells* radio.

"You like this station, too?"

"Sometimes they play our song," she mused.

india

DECEMBER *30, 2021*

My alarm rang out softly, on low volume because I was buried under a heavy duvet and locked in the arms of a deeply slumbering man. I reached for it and turned it off quickly, so I didn't wake Malik.

The whirlwind of reuniting with the love of my life should have felt unnerving and uncomfortable, and the ease with which we'd settled right back into each other's comfort zones alarmingly fast.

On the contrary, I felt off when I wasn't with him at the studio, or he didn't come by my place. Like there was a place I should be, but I wasn't.

That feeling of displacement disappeared when I knew I was going to see him, or we were together.

I still enjoyed my time of quiet and solitude. When Malik slept, it wasn't for long, so I got up, knowing I'd only have a brief window of time to myself. I wiggled out of his grasp, watching to see if I'd disturbed his sleep enough to wake him, but he only sucked in a long, loud breath through his nose. I pulled the curtains to darken the room again and headed to the bathroom to take care of my morning routine, then headed to the kitchen.

I stopped to turn the lights on the tree. I noticed, underneath it, an oblong box that wasn't there before. We had agreed that we wouldn't put each other through the awkwardness of exchanging gifts for the holiday. It was enough to spend as much time together as possible before the new year.

Tonight was my father's birthday party and Malik's semi-official reveal. I had been ducking indirect questions about him and I was excited to re-introduce him.

December was never slow for retail, so I monitored my laptop, open on the counter, and got busy in the kitchen. It wasn't long before I heard the rustle of bedcovers and the shuffle of bare feet on the carpet. I tried not to listen and imagine what Malik was doing in the en-suite bathroom before the door opened again and he appeared in the hallway, bare chested in soft cotton lounge pants. They did nothing to hide the state of his morning arousal.

He didn't seem to mind me openly watching him as he rounded the center island to drop a kiss on my cheek, then my lips. He was still bleary-eyed and deliciously scruffy— and I loved him that way— but his minty fresh breath warmed my skin.

"Hey Lover. Good morning."

"Mmmmm...Hey, Lover. A good morning it is." He ran a hand up the side of my body, stopping to cup my breast through the thick terry-cloth robe I wore. "I gotta share you today?"

"I have work to do, but I don't have to go into the office.

The party isn't until tonight, so we can relax. You want coffee?"

"Please." He watched me pour two mugs of strong, black coffee and slide one over to him. "What do I smell?"

I pointed to the double oven that I was putting to good use. His brows rose at the sight of croissants rising in the top and bacon cooking in the bottom. I'd just finished scrambling cheesy eggs to build our breakfast sandwiches and toasted freezer hash browns.

"Let's wake up over on the couch while breakfast finishes cooking," I suggested.

I settled in, tucking my legs up under me. He detoured to the tree to pick up the box he'd left there, then joined me, scooting close.

"I can't wait one more second for you to open this," he said, handing the box to me and taking my mug of coffee. "I've actually had this for years. Meant to send it to you, but I chickened out."

"I noticed you slipped me a little something."

"Ima slip you a lot of something later. Open it."

He brought his mug to his lips and watched with eager eyes as I ripped the festive wrapping from the box, then sliced my fingernail through the tape holding it closed.

When I flipped open the box, my mouth fell open. "Malik... you did not..."

"I wanted you to have it."

I dug into the box, freeing a matte black frame. Enclosed was an autographed cover of my favorite album— LL Cool J, Mr. Smith. Next to it was a maxi single promo CD from Def Jam records, including the radio cut of my favorite — *our* favorite song, *Hey Lover* and the instrumental version, also signed.

"I... this is..." I swallowed the lump in my throat and blinked back a swell of tears. "Oh, my... Malik."

"I did real good, huh? You can't even say whole sentences," he joked.

I laughed, grateful for levity because I was overwhelmed. "I just didn't expect..."

I laughed again, obviously unable to utter a coherent sentence, so I flung my arms around his neck, almost spilling our coffee before he could set the mugs on the table in front of us. His arms closed around me, holding me tight up against him.

I fought the tears as long as I could, but I couldn't hold them back when I heard him whisper in my ear. "I love you, India. Again. Still. I have never stopped loving you."

I hadn't planned to let those words cross my lips for a while. I knew when I opened the door and he was standing there that my feelings for him hadn't changed, but I was.... afraid.

So afraid that he would disappear again, that it would be too much, I'd love too hard, and it would scare him.

Malik's gift was special. His confession that his feelings hadn't waned either gave me the push I needed.

"I really missed you, Malik. I feel like part of my life has been on hold, waiting for you. Having you back has been like pressing play again. I love you, still. I love you again. Don't.... please don't leave me again."

"I'm here," he said, pulling back. He cupped my face in his hands and kissed me. "I'm staying right here."

"What is all this stuff?" Malik asked, as I loaded him down with two large, heavy gift bags to take down to the car. I picked up my purse and a smaller gift bag and followed him out of the door. "Is this all for your dad? For his birthday?"

"Well, we're also celebrating his retirement, so there are a few extra gifts to encourage him to lean into relaxation. Golf balls and running shoes, things like that. Junie got him a new tennis racquet so they can play at their club."

I pulled the door shut and locked it. We shuffled down the hall quietly with our bags in tow.

"A tennis racquet? Golf accessories? I'm feeling like whiskey glasses isn't going to cut it. I just don't want to look like I went cheap."

"They're personalized Oakmont Whiskey glasses. He'll love them and they'll look great on his wet bar. You ready?"

He picked up the overflowing bag and nodded. "Let's go."

We loaded up the car and rode through Atlanta's post-Christmas sale traffic to my parent's two-story brick colonial in Sandy Springs, an in-town Atlanta suburb. The circular drive was already packed with cars, but I skillfully maneuvered into a space.

"I just realized I haven't been to your folks' place in a long time. Looks the same."

"I know I pushed you to come, but you really don't have to go in here if you don't want to."

"I'm good," he assured me. "How do I look?"

I checked out his fit, giving an approving glance at the long-sleeved, open collar black-and-white checkered shirt. He wore a black vest over it, paired it with dark jeans and his black slip-on sneakers with white trim and soles. He'd gone to the barber earlier for a touch up to his haircut and a beard trim. His eyes were bright, his smile timid.

"You look nervous. Relax." I leaned over the center

console and kissed him. "And sexy. I already can't wait until this party is over so we can go home."

We joined the crowd in the house, dropping off our bags near the mountain of presents in the foyer. The formal living room and adjoining great room had, as usual, been transformed.

"I forgot how y'all have a hundred trees every year," said Malik, his eyes roving the fully dressed Christmas trees around the house.

"Junie has become what you'd call a Christmas maximist. She does not believe a home can ever have too many trees."

The main tree was still in the foyer, taller and grander than ever. It was flocked, decorated with silver, gold and red ornaments and pretty pearl lights.

I heard a light rustle and noticed a few limbs on the tree shaking. I bent to peer between the branches and laughed. "Get out of the tree, you little gremlins!" I shouted into it.

Two gray balls of fur came tumbling from underneath and scattered. "Those are the new kittens, George and Louise. We're not allowed to call her Weezy... but we do."

"Are those cats in that tree again? I can't wait until we take that thing down."

I heard my father approaching, then saw him round the bend. Retirement looked so good on him— even the crow's feet around his eyes seemed to have disappeared. His dark skin glowed, his beard was extra silver, and he looked dapper in a tailored black suit.

"Oh, good, you're here," he said to me. But his eyes were on Malik.

"Happy birthday, Dad." I brushed his cheek with my lips. "Looks like the party is off to a great start. You remember Malik?"

"Mr. Bronson," he said, stepping forward to shake his hand. "It's great to see you again- and happy birthday. You're looking well."

"Glad you could join us, son. Would you mind helping Isaac and Junie with the bags of ice in the kitchen? I believe they could use some muscle. I need a word with India."

Malik glanced at me. I assured him with a nod. I knew what this chat was going to be about.

As soon as he was out of earshot, the polite smile disappeared. "Now, you know I don't get into your personal business—"

"Don't tell that lie. You were just about to. I know you liked Tony, but it didn't work out with him. Malik and I have reconnected, and we decided we want to give it another shot. So, you can not like Malik or us being back together all you want. It won't change a thing."

Dad's mouth opened, then closed, then opened and closed again. Then he laughed. "I was just going to ask if this man is who you want? Who you're happy with?"

"It is. He's nervous that you don't like him."

He nodded in the direction of the kitchen. "Don't tell him I said this, but I liked that one a lot. I only put up with Tony because I thought you liked him. I hope you two got it right this time."

"Me too, Dad. For now, I'm happy."

"Keep it that way. And when you're not happy, move along." He waited to make sure I caught his pointed stare. "Time goes by too fast to waste it. Do you hear me?"

I hugged him, squeezing him tight. "I hear you."

"Now tell me, what's the latest at Parker? How is first quarter outlook coming?"

I knew he saw my eyes roll, but he didn't care. "You can take the man out of the business—"

"Can't take the business out of the man. Speak to me."

WHEN INDIA SAID BRONSON'S BIRTHDAY PARTY GOT WILD, SHE WAS not exaggerating...it was all the way live.

The house was packed with people. A DJ set up in one corner, spinning records and sending music bumping through every speaker. In another part of the house, the bar was open, and four bartenders were hopping, struggling to keep glasses full. I was grateful that I didn't drink since the line to order was three rows deep.

I wandered around with a bottle of cold water, quickly tiring of trying to keep India in sight. She was in her *daughter of the host and CEO* bag, floating from one group to another to smile, laugh, joke. Ugh.

I stepped onto a second-floor patio overlooking the lush backyard that bordered a golf course. The evening air was chilly, but two huge heaters pumped out warm air at each end, so I posted up near one. This party was a testament to my love for India. Only for her would I endure this much people-ing.

Steena approached in a strapless red dress and a silky shoulder-length bob with blunt bangs. "Checking on you," she said and handed me a glass of something dark. "It's sparkling grape juice. India told me you don't drink. Thought you'd want something besides water."

I took the glass and sucked down a gulp of sweet, fizzy juice. "I just needed a minute. There are a lot of people here."

Her lips bent into a smile, but the smile didn't reach her eyes. "Don't do crowds much?"

"Tech life is pretty solitary. Dark rooms and monitors mostly."

"Mmmmm. I see." Steena sucked in her cheeks and gave me a slow, pandering nod. Her expression said she was on a mission.

"Is it time to make the speech? The one where I'd better not hurt India like I did before, or else?"

"Hurt?" She huffed a humorless laugh. "You did more than hurt her. You destroyed her. It took her years to get over you and even then, she settled for...*Tony*."

She cringed. I wanted to join her but didn't dare.

"I actively hate what you did to her, Malik."

"I understand. I would hate me too."

"Oh, spare me the self-deprecating, *I'd hate me too* bull-shit act. I just thought you should know that seven years ago, she had to talk me out of locating you so we could have a *chat*. If I have to drag her through another heartache because of you, she will not be able to stop me this time. Have I made myself clear?"

I swallowed hard. She was tall already and with her heels on, we saw eye to eye. Her stare was piercing. And unavoidable.

'Yes ma'am," I replied. "Loud and clear. Understood."

"Good." She painted on a wide, bright smile, then guzzled a mouth full of wine and audibly swallowed. "You will never find a woman like India ever again. Don't fuck this up."

"I'm trying really hard not to."

A middle-aged man wandered out onto the patio, his jacket rumpled, drink in hand.

Steena groaned, rolling her eyes. "Ugh, I can't take this guy," she mumbled.

"Who is that?"

"Quinn. He runs business development for Parker."

"Kristeena," the man said, weaving in our direction, disdain dripping from his tone. "Of course, you're here. Any opportunity to hang out with the Parkers, right?"

"Let's try to be civil tonight, Quinn. Can we do that?"

"Mmmmh." He waved in my direction. "Is this... is this your man? How do you like dating a woman almost taller n' you?"

"Quinn, this is Malik. He's India's guest. He works in... technology."

I leaned forward with an outstretched hand. He shook it, albeit loosely.

"Technology. That's like... like saying business." He chuckled at his own joke. "What's that mean?"

"We do a lot of things, but mainly we write video games."

"Oh! Okay, yeah. You... you should help India with that gaming project she's working on."

"Quinn!" Steena blurted, stepping between us and sliding a hand around his forearm. "Why don't we head over this way..."

"What gaming project?" I asked, moving around her.

"Gaming...websites. You...y' know anything about that? Gaming?"

I glanced around him at Steena. She stared back with wide eyes and a guilty expression. "I know a lot about that."

"Quinn, let's find you a seat. And some water. Did you get a ride here?"

My jaw clenched tight, watching Steena guide him by the shoulders to the padded benches that lined the patio, lit by twinkling lights. As soon as their backs were turned, I stalked into the house, headed right for India, mid-conversation, glass of wine aloft.

"Sorry to interrupt," I said, gripping India's arm. "I need to talk to you."

Before she could argue or apologize to the guests, I whisked her away. An empty room in a house full of people was a tall order, so I pulled her back to the patio.

She yanked her arm from my grasp and stepped back. "What is wrong? Did someone say something to you?"

"When were you going to tell me about the game platform you're building at Parker?"

Her mouth dropped open, and I watched her expression change. The look of surprise, then guilt, then dread. "The—the what?"

I seethed. "Do not... don't pretend you don't know what I'm talking about. How long have you been planning shit behind my back?"

"I've not been *planning shit* behind your back! Who told you?"

"Does it matter? No one told *me*. It was something I spoke to you about, and now it's something you're working on. And I'm just wondering how long this was going to go on before you said something to me about it."

Steena appeared next to India. "It was Quinn. He's drunk. I'm sorry. He just spit it out—"

"Steena knows. People on your staff know. But I don't

know. Are you doing the same shit I told you I didn't want you to do? I don't need you to rescue me."

"I'm not trying to, if you would let me explain!"

"Explain what? How you're building exactly what I said I needed without talking to me about it?"

"What's happening out here?" Bronson stepped onto the patio. He'd shed his jacket and his whiskey, and his shirt was unbuttoned at the collar. His eyes bounced around the half circle from me to Steena and India and back.

"Nothing, Dad. It's just... a disagreement."

"Well, your disagreement is drawing eyes and ears. I don't want this distraction."

"A disagreement?" I questioned. "A disagreement is a difference of opinion. This is you throwing on a cape to rescue my company and I don't need that. If you would have talked to me about this, I would have told you that."

"Like you wouldn't have shot the entire idea down without even listening."

"What idea?" Bronson asked. "We haven't discussed anything new. And why is it public knowledge?"

"Ask your friend Quinn," said Steena, "who can't hold his liquor or his mouth."

"If everyone would shut up and let me speak!"

Silence fell over the small crowd. India was red in the face, her lips curled.

"I am in preliminary, early planning stages of launching a game platform. It's not an original idea, but... yes, it is the result of a conversation with Malik. I want to target Black creators and consumers. Maybe we can't compete with the big dogs, but we could carve out a niche space where creators could flourish and have a spot to publish their games without being taken advantage of."

Bronson crossed his arms over his chest and widened his stance. "And? What does the research say?"

"Still in progress. I gave the project to Quinn weeks ago and I don't know how we're arguing about it now, but... I planned to offer Malik's company the first slot."

"Without telling me about it," I added. "Just pop up with an idea we talked about in private and expect me to be fine with it."

"Malik... baby, I promise I was not hiding it from you. I knew you would assume it was for you and about you, but it's bigger than you. If we find that it's something we can make work, we'll move forward with or without Hines Tech, but—"

"It'll be without Hines Tech. I don't need charity from Parker."

"Malik." India paused, moving closer and dropping her tone. "Can we talk about this later? Now is not the time or the place, and I'll be able to have a robust discussion when we—"

"Mr. Parker, thank you for your hospitality." I clapped a confused Bronson on the shoulder. "Please extend my apologies to your wife that I can't stay longer."

"Malik. You don't have to leave."

I stormed away, fuming and ready to explode.

"No! India, he needs time. Let him chill out," I heard Steena tell her.

Yeah. Let me chill. All the way out.

The anger had fizzled quickly while I stood outside in

the driveway to wait for my car. I felt betrayed, like I exposed my vulnerabilities to a person who, just that morning, had told me she loved me over and over... while plotting to exploit me behind my back.

I didn't want to think the worst of India. In fact, I hated to. But my heart was too wounded to not assume the worst-case scenario.

Why else would she be pumping me for information every time I talked about the game? I thought it was so endearing that she'd asked so many questions, wanting to understand my world.

Was that why she'd run a background check?

The car dropped me at the studio. I unlocked the doors and walked through, my footsteps echoing around the space. It was dark and forlorn, and I was afraid that we might be in danger of staying that way.

I passed the kitchen, the remnants of Brandon's party a few nights ago still strewn about. Bottles of liquor lined the countertops, the trash and recycling bins were both full, and the room smelled like a distillery.

I scanned the bottles, looking for anything that sounded familiar. I hadn't had a drink in so long that the terminologies, the alcohol content, the good brands had all fallen from my mind.

"Fuck it," I mumbled to myself. I grabbed a bottle of bourbon by the neck and headed to the stairs. Once I reached the loft, I slammed the door shut and began tearing off my clothes. The buttons on the shirt I bought specifically for the party ricocheted around the room.

I kicked off my shoes and left my jeans where they landed when I stepped out of them, then laid across the bed.

Stared at the ceiling.

Drank bourbon right from the bottle. The bite as it hit my throat, then the warmth and numbness it brought—feelings, heart, thoughts, words—was exactly what I was looking for.

I pulled out my phone, called up the Spotify app, and played a familiar tune.

"*Hey, loverrrr. This issss more than a crushhhh,*" I sang to myself.

I only knew I passed out there because the incessant pounding on my door and buzzing of my phone woke me up.

CHAPTER EIGHTEEN

india

"Dammit, Malik! Open the fucking door!"

I'd been pounding on the door, thick with layers of white paint, for at least ten minutes, alternating with back-to-back calls, all of which were going to voicemail. I didn't even count the texts that I'd been sending since an hour after he'd left the party.

Since it was the first year in my new role, I couldn't just disappear from an event because my boyfriend stomped off in an angry tantrum. Dad made it clear that he expected me to remain at the party, smile and nod, schmooze and drink with his guests. So I spent the evening pretending.

Pretending to care, pretending to be happy and festive, pretending I wasn't worried that a brief reunion with Malik was ill-fated and would end the same way it ended seven years ago. This time, our split would be my fault.

I joined the family for the annual roast and toast of Bronson Parker. As soon as the punch hit my throat, I made my apologies and my exit, ran to my car and headed straight for Malik's studio.

I gave the door another half dozen thumps. No response.

"Fuck!" I screamed into the night air and pounded on the door. I pulled out my phone and dialed his number again. And left another message.

"Malik, I'm sorry. I'm. *Sorry*. Jesus, you're so... fucking sensitive!"

I sniffed, feeling the tears build behind my eyes and wanting to quench them, but it was late, and I was tired and tipsy and I didn't have the strength to keep them at bay.

"Look... yes, okay. I should have said something to you. I know that now. But I had to make sure we could build it and the platform would work and I didn't sound stupid before I brought the idea to you. I hate that you think—"

I sobbed, finding it hard to catch my breath. I slid down the door and planted myself on the step.

"I'll dump the idea if you want me to. I will. I want you in my life more than I care about this project. Please open the door, baby. Please..."

I ran out of time, and the call disconnected.

I was shivering in the cold, crying on the front step of a warehouse at 3 AM in a questionable area of town. If the Business Chronicle could see me now— ATLANTA CEO DUMPED BY BOYFRIEND, FOUND CRYING IN THE STREET. I wanted to laugh at the imaginary but realistic headline.

Behind my head, the lock slid out of place with the scrape of rusted metal on metal. I scrambled to get on all fours, then stand as the door swung open. Malik stood in the entryway in his briefs and nothing else, his phone in one hand.

"India."

His voice was a gravel pit. Fresh tears stung my eyes when he didn't greet me with *Hey, Lover.* "Guess I'll get that message eventually."

"There are a few," I replied, sniffling. "And a lot of texts."

He glanced at his phone, his face illuminated in the glow. "Yeah. I see that."

"It's cold, and it's the middle of the night. Can I come in?"

He stepped aside. I walked past him into the studio. There was a different energy in the building—not warm, sexy, welcoming. It was cool and dark. And there was... a smell.

I eyed the bottles of liquor, empty beer cans and cups lining the counter, all on display since Malik had turned on the overhead lights. His eyes were bloodshot and his skin sallow.

"Have you been drinking?" I asked.

"Yes," he answered, quicker and more direct than I had expected.

"I... thought you didn't drink anymore."

"I haven't in a while. But I was *distraught.*" He paused and stared, I guessed to make sure I heard him. "The team had a party here. I grabbed a bottle that only had a couple of swallows left. I'm a lightweight, anyway. Knocked me out."

"Malik, I'm—"

"Sorry. I know. I heard. I read it in your texts."

"You say that like I'm not really sorry. You keep saying

you still know me; you know me so well. Look at my face and tell me I'm not sorry."

"I didn't say you weren't sorry. I said I know. I heard you."

"You heard me. And...."

"And...being sorry doesn't make this okay. I put trust in you, I was vulnerable with you, I shared things with you that I was hopeful for—"

"Things I could help you with!" I blurted, interrupting him. "You've built a great thing, but you can't get to the next thing by yourself. You run from help like you don't deserve it, especially if it would come from me."

"I told you exactly what I was looking for. And instead of talking it out with me, you took that information to open a project at your company." He paused, letting his words land hard on my ear. "You set out to risk money, your reputation, your position to put it behind..."

He waved a loose hand around. "This? Is... is that why you ran a background check on me? I saw that, by the way. Did you need to see if I'd be worth the investment?"

I knew I should have fed that bullshit report to the shredder.

"I did not run a background check on you. I know you, and what I don't know, I could ask. Tony ran that report and brought it to my office after GameBox."

"Then why was it in your bag and not at your office. You brought it home to read, to check me out, right?"

"No, Malik. It's in my bag because I didn't want anyone at Parker to get their hands on it before I was ready to launch my first client."

His Adam's apple bobbed several times as he swallowed. And stared. Was he trying to figure out of I was lying? Making excuses?

"Also…why not *this*? I'm sorry, Malik. I went about this the wrong way, but is this not your dream, your life's work, what you'd rather be doing more than anything else? Why would I not put faith in you, and money and effort behind making something happen for you? This *is* what you need, right? This would put you on?"

It took him what felt like a long span of time to respond. "It would open a lot of doors, yeah."

"If it wasn't from me, right? I can be your beautiful girlfriend, your scenery, somebody to play games with, but not your business partner. I can't use the same savvy that pushed my company to its best performance in years for you, but I can spread my legs and let you fuck me. Is that the only reason you came back? Is that all you ever wanted from me?"

"Stop. You know it's not. I'm just not looking for someone to throw a bunch of money at my problems."

"Bullshit!" I shot back. "That's exactly what you're looking for. If a company reached out to you tomorrow, offering to host your game, let you retain ownership and license the game stick, you'd cry. You'd throw a party. But if it's me, it's a problem. And *that's* a red flag, Malik. You don't trust that I care enough about you, your company, your dream, your game—"

"I don't trust *me*!" He exploded, pounding his fist into his chest. "If it fails, *you* fail! Then it's a Domino effect. It's critical articles in the paper, and Bronson is looking at me sideways and your staff, who aren't even loyal enough to keep a potential project a secret, starts planning to remove you as head of the company. I don't want that on my head."

"That would never happen, Malik."

"You don't know that, India." Malik crossed the room, stopping to stand in front of me. "I won't gamble your future on my dream. I'll risk another company's money because I'm not in love with their CEO."

"But... what if *I* trust *you*?"

I reached for him, and he came closer. Emboldened, I dared myself to touch him, and he let me, leaning into my palm when I caressed his cheek and the wild hairs in his beard.

"What if I know a good idea when I hear it, and I think this idea has legs? What if you just need some force behind you? And what if you had a hand in making sure it can't fail?"

"Nothing is fail proof."

"Just listen. I want you to hire an attorney— preferably not Tony Clark — to write a deal that contracts you to develop this platform. For *you*. If you can show us how it should work with Hines Tech, then duplicate that process over and over, then Parker won't have any issue making an investment. Nobody knows what you need better than you."

I felt him wrestling inside himself. It made perfect sense for him to be involved and it was the only way I was going to get him on board. I just needed him to see it.

"Think about it. You'd get funds to keep Hines Tech going, to research and build the platform the way you want it to run. A wide-open space to publish your games and they stay yours. Parker recoups our investment on the back end. That's how we do business. Write a deal that's fair and I'll sign it. It could work, right?"

"It could work," he finally admitted. "But you said you wanted to be... regular. Not India, CEO with me. You wanted to be able to take all of this off and just... be you. Now you want me to work for you—"

"With me," I corrected. "An this *is* me, Malik. This is

who I am, who I have always been. When it comes to you getting what you want, making your dreams come true, if I can make it happen, it's *going* to happen. You came back to me for a reason. You were better, different. So, let's be better, different together. Partner with me and we can grow Hines Tech and Parker Games as big as you can dream."

Malik moved in close, then ran his hands down my body and gripped my thighs, lifting me up onto the island. He stepped between my legs and pulled me up against him. "So, what if…"

"What if?" I prodded, as I slid my arms around him.

"What if Bronson hates the idea?"

"Bronson doesn't run Parker. I do. He's your girlfriend's dad, and nothing more. And he told me not to tell you this, but… he likes you."

Malik smiled for the first time since I'd walked in the door. The way his face lost all its tightness and worry, I felt like I was chipping away at the wall he'd thrown up. The wall that had, actually, always been there.

"That's what's up," he said. "Do I have to work with that Quinn guy?"

"Uh, no." I sighed. "The part I hate about being a leader is knowing when to dismiss a person and… that time has come. We'll spin it as early retirement or say he's going to seek other opportunities. You work with me, and me alone. Deal?"

"Deal," he agreed. Finally.

I relaxed, my shoulders sagging in relief. I pulled him to me and wrapped my arms around him. "I'm so sorry for how this came out. But I'm so thankful right now… that I don't have to stop Steena from trying to hurt you."

He laughed, probably only because he was thankful for that, too.

"I missed you," he whispered. "I wanted to be with you tonight."

"I'm here now." I leaned in, dropping a kiss on his lips. "And I don't have to go anywhere. But can I make a suggestion?"

"I will take any suggestion you have, CEO."

"You smell like you took a sweaty nap in a brewery—"

"That was not a suggestion, India." He laughed and tried to step back, but I locked my legs around him.

"I wasn't done! Let's go get in the shower. And then get in the bed. And then start planning, because we haven't even started talking about how that stick is the most amazing thing ever and I want to be the first to license it. I want to sell it in the mall kiosks."

"Like I said, I take all suggestions from you."

He tightened his arms around me and picked me up, then started moving toward the staircase. I squealed, holding on tight. As soon as we hit the landing upstairs, I hopped down and ran for the shower. I turned it on and switched the temperature to hot.

Malik took his time following. He shed his briefs and kicked them off, then joined me in the bathroom where the room was filling with steam.

The bathroom was small, built for one, so a joint shower required a choreography, but we had it down to a science. I always got in first, got us started, and he came in behind me.

I stepped into the enclosed space, letting the water cascade over my body and lathered up a bath puff. I felt Malik's hands on my waist as he stepped in behind me. I handed him the puff and held my hands out, bracing against the wall. Malik rubbed the puff across my skin, gently scrubbing every inch from my neck to my feet. Then detouring to slide his fingers between my legs, gently teasing my clit to attention.

I leaned back against his chest, giving him room to work soapy hands over my soft belly, up to my breasts. He took his time caressing my skin, playing with my nipples, laying soft kisses across my cheek.

"I'm sorry," he said.

"I know." I turned his face so I could kiss him. "You've got no more times to run away from me, Malik Hines. I will hunt you down every time. We're doing this together. You got that?"

He rinsed the puff and squeezed the water over my body to rinse the suds down the drain. "How did the party end?"

"Oh, it's still going," I replied with a laugh. "But it'll probably end the same way it always ends—my dad leading the Electric Slide through the living room in his socks."

I felt his laughter rumbling through his chest. "I was looking forward to that this year. But I'm glad I'm not missing this."

He slid one hand back down my body. My hips bucked at the sensation of fingers swirling and circling my clit, pressing then teasing, taking me higher.

I whimpered, mentally begging him not to stop.

He teased and kissed and played with my nipples and echoed my moans until a wave of pleasure overtook me. I almost lost my balance, but he had me in a tight grip and held me close.

"I want you inside me. Please, Malik..."

He turned me around, pulling me up against his wet body, and lifted a leg to hook it over his hip.

I writhed against him as he buried himself inside me,

trying not to lose balance in the slip of the water beneath our feet. My muffled cries against his shoulder grew louder as he pounded his body against mine. I loved the sounds bouncing off the tile. I gyrated my hips, squirming, pushed to the edge.

"God, I'm coming. Come with me!"

With little warning, he stiffened, his fingertips digging deep into my skin. I cried out, trembling and convulsing. I felt him spasm, heard him gasp and grunt in climax. Then held tight as his muscles relaxed.

"*That* is how you do makeup sex."

"Almost worth the soreness later," Malik joked. He turned me, making sure I was steady. "It is too damn small in this shower and I'm losing hot water. I'll finish up and meet you in bed."

"Fine," I pouted, hanging up my bath puff and sliding the shower door open. "It's too cramped in here, anyway."

"Hey, Lover..."

Those words I'd been longing to hear, and still hadn't heard enough to make up for how much I'd missed them, stopped me in my tracks. I turned back to him.

"Yeah?"

"I love you. Thank you for loving me like you do. I realize now that I'm in a relationship with a woman that wants to be a partner. I want that too... good and bad, up and down, salaried and hourly. For.... forever."

"Took you long enough to come around. I love you too."

CHAPTER NINETEEN

September 24, 2022

"It's on! It's on! Hurry! Move over."

India squeezed between me and Brandon in front of the TV in the studio lounge. Months of hard work had culminated in a long but wildly exciting day at the official launch of Parker Games, featuring the Galaxy of Games. The team would get to see themselves become famous... sort of. A local news team had spent launch day with us.

"I'm Caroline Thompson with Team 6 News, coming to you from Edgewood Mall, where Parker Enterprises made another huge splash. Today, gamers young and old could not be more excited about the launch of Parker Games and their first offering, Galaxy Bros."

The camera panned to a kiosk in the center of the mall, stocked with rows of Galaxy Games cards and Play Anywhere Game Sticks. As more games were developed and released, they would be added to the platform that we designed and launched with Parker and would allow unlimited access to the games in the series.

"Looking *nice!*" Corey yelled from the back of the room, pumping his fists in the air.

Corey graduated from Morehouse earlier in the year with a job. With Brandon spending most of his time on the Parker Games platform, it made sense to promote Corey to fill in the gaps. He was our lead developer and would spearhead the next game in the series.

Rebekah, our recently minted Chief of Design, rolled past the reporter, a tablet on her lap detailing the schematics of how the display should be set up. She shouted instructions to the team manning the two larger-than-life screens, and the games attached to them. Players crowded around both TVs. It was rowdy... and a ton of fun.

Launch day was a rite of passage and my favorite part of being a game developer. Watching people play for the first time, explore, find the secret passages and special prize, then win each level was the best part.

"Today marks the beginning of a new era for Parker Enterprises, whose CEO had this to say when we spoke to her earlier..."

The feed switched to a pre-recorded interview with India. It had been taped early that morning, right after we gained access to the mall and could load in. As usual, she was poised in front of the camera— a bright, gorgeous smile, deep brown eyes that saw into your soul, and a sparkling personality that drew her to people.

People like me.

Hey, Lover.

"The team at Parker has been hard at work bringing this platform to the market. The goal was to foster an atmosphere where independent developers feel welcome to publish their games, where they're going to earn fair royalties without exorbi-

tant hosting fees, and where consumers can play engaging games at reasonable prices. That begins with this incredibly fun suite of games from Hines Tech called Galaxy Bros. I am personally addicted to Mercury and Venus, and I know gamers are looking forward to what comes next from our partner, Hines Tech. Parker is proud to be Atlanta's source for storage, convenience, retail, repair and now?" She turned to wave a hand to the crew in the background. "Entertainment."

"You look good on TV, baby," I told India, pulling her close to me and dropping a kiss on her temple.

"I do, don't it?"

"Shhh!" Brandon hissed.

"Well, congratulations on a great launch. Galaxy Day at the Mall looks to be a huge hit. Can you give us a hint at what's coming down the pipeline?"

India smiled into the camera. "Let's just say that I see a lot of..." She paused to wink. "Adventures in store for us."

The screen switched to recorded scenes of players gathered around the TVs and the building crowd around them.

Brandon turned down the volume and tossed the remote to the coffee table. "We packed that place out. Everybody had a ball."

"Launch day owes me nothing," I agreed. "Nothing crashed, there were no bugs—" I gave Brandon a fist bump. "And I think the sales numbers are going to be good after the weekend. Great job everybody!"

The room filled with cheers and applause. I pushed myself up from the couch and pulled India up with me.

"Aight' y'all. It's been a good one, but a long one. You ain't got to home, but you got to get out of my house."

"How are you kicking us out of the office?" Brandon asked.

"Because I live here. It's my birthday and I have plans." I

grinned at India. She winked in return. "So, I want everyone out of here in five minutes, and I don't want to see anybody in here over the weekend. We need a Mars release before the end of the year. Corey has an aggressive schedule, so watch your email, alright?"

"Yeah, we're hitting it hard next week, so be ready."

"You heard the man. Enjoy a few days off. Last one out, lock the deadbolt. Good night."

I pulled India through the studio and up the stairs to the loft.

The door wasn't even closed all the way before I dragged her to me and crushed my mouth to hers. Our tongues swirled, fighting for dominance while we shuffled around the room. When we were close enough to the bed, I wrapped my arm around her waist and pulled her down on top of me.

She sat up, giggling as she straddled me. "Hey, Lover."

"Hey, Lover," I replied, as I always did.

"I'm so... *so* happy for you. Launch went very well. I just want you to be happy— it's the best birthday present."

"*You* are the best birthday present. I got to see my dream come to life. My team got to be on the news— they're never gonna forget that. I can't even tell you what you've done for Hines Tech. And for me."

"Since your success means my success, it was a good day for me, too."

She turned her head, pausing to listen. Then a sultry smile slowly crossed her lips. "I don't hear anything," she whispered. "Sounds like we're alone. Now you can really show me how much you appreciate me."

A low growl rumbled in my throat. I rolled us over and sat up, leering at her shapely body in skintight jeans and a long-sleeved Galaxy Bros t-shirt. "Say less. I'm about to appreciate the fuck out of you."

"That is why you kicked everybody out, isn't it?"

I pulled off my Galaxy Bros t-shirt and tossed it into the closet hamper, then pulled off my jeans. I scooped up the pile of clothing India left and added them to the hamper.

"It's been a real good day, but all I want is to be deep inside you. I've been waiting all day to choose my birthday adventure."

I wiggled my brows at her, sure I saw her blush.

India scooted back to the headboard, up against the pillows. I remembered a time when I was afraid that she'd one day she'd wake up and realize that we lived different lives on different levels, that she still wasn't with someone that was good enough for her.

She was smiling and relaxed, as comfortable with me in my space as she had ever been. Like she belonged and had always been there.

Reuniting with India was like regrowing a missing body part and learning how to use it again. Forgetting all that bullshit about being even and living the same life. We bridged the gaps, wherever they showed up, together. As partners, we did far more— and did it better— than we'd ever be able to do alone.

I still hadn't made up for all the time we'd lost when I didn't know that that's how you love somebody... but we were working on it.

I must have been frozen, entranced by her for too long, because India squinted at me and asked, "Are you writing a game right now?"

I grinned. "Maybe. Why?"

"Because I have..." Her eyes lit up. "...*ideas.*"

For as long as I can remember, I would rather be in my bedroom reading and writing than doing anything else, but I began seriously pursuing a writing career in 2011.

I love coffee and Sunday Brunch. On the weekend, you'll probably find me near water and if I'm lucky, on an ocean beach with my kindle, Tangy Mae, digging my toes into sugar-white sand.

By day I am an Executive Administrative Assistant at an Atlanta beverage giant. By night, when I'm not writing books, I'm devouring them. Visit my website at at Booksby-dlwhite.com

For VIP news and free stuff, join my newsletter at Books bydlwhite.com/newsletter

also by dl white

Thank you for reading this novel. I appreciate your support more than you know. If you enjoyed it, I hope you'll drop a review at your fave retail site and Goodreads. Read my books in ebook, print or in audio (select titles) at *Booksbylwhite.com/books.*

Brunch at Ruby's

Dinner at Sam's: A Ruby's Novel (Ruby's 2)

Beach Thing

Leslie's Curl & Dye (Potter Lake Small Town Romance 1)

Second Time Around (Potter Lake Small Town Romance 2/ Holiday shorts)

The Guy Next Door (Potter Lake Small Town Romance 3)

A Thin Line

The Never List

Unexpected (Holiday short)

The Kwanzaa Brunch (Holiday short)

www.ingramcontent.com/pod-product-compliance
Lightning Source LLC
Chambersburg PA
CBHW022005170726
47994CB00022B/2048